Putney and the Magic eyePad

Book 1

MK Tufft

PUTNEY
DESIGNS

Putney Designs LLC
West Chester, Ohio, USA

This is a work of fiction. Names, characters, places and incidents are products of the author's imagination or are used fictitiously. Any resemblance to actual events or locales or persons, living or dead, is entirely coincidental.

Text and Illustrations copyright © 2020 MK Tufft
Published by Putney Designs, LLC, West Chester, Ohio, USA

For orders, please visit www.putneydesigns.com

All rights reserved.

No part of this publication may be reproduced, distributed, or transmitted in any form or by any means, including photocopying, recording, or other electronic or mechanical methods, without the prior written permission of the publisher, except in the case of brief quotations embodied in reviews and certain other noncommercial uses permitted by copyright law.

The moral right of the author and illustrator has been asserted.

Cover illustration by Anastasia Kosataya,
VisualArt Studio
Interior illustrations & photos by MK Tufft

Hardback ISBN-13: 978-1-7346636-2-4
Paperback ISBN-13: 978-1-7346636-1-7
eBook ISBN-13: 978-1-7346636-0-0

Library of Congress Control Number: 2020903146

Want more project details? STEM experiments you can do at home? Please visit my website. Plus, sign up for my newsletter to receive **exclusive character sketches** of characters from my books!

www.putneydesigns.com
www.putneydesigns.com/subscribe

Also by MK Tufft

Putney and the Magic eyePad
Book 1

The Cardboard Boat Race
Putney and the Magic eyePad–Book 2

The Butterfly Detective
Putney and the Magic eyePad–Book 3

For Mom, who raised me to believe I could do anything.

In memory of Dad, who taught me so much about the design process, especially manufacturing and practical considerations, like how to get that custom-built desk through a doorway.

For my husband, Stephen, who always lets me be my own person, no matter how messy that is.

For my very creative older sister, Janet, who inspired me in so many ways.

For my cover illustrator, Anastasia Kosataya, who did an amazing job of bringing Putney and Sam to life!

Map of Putney's Palmetto Dunes

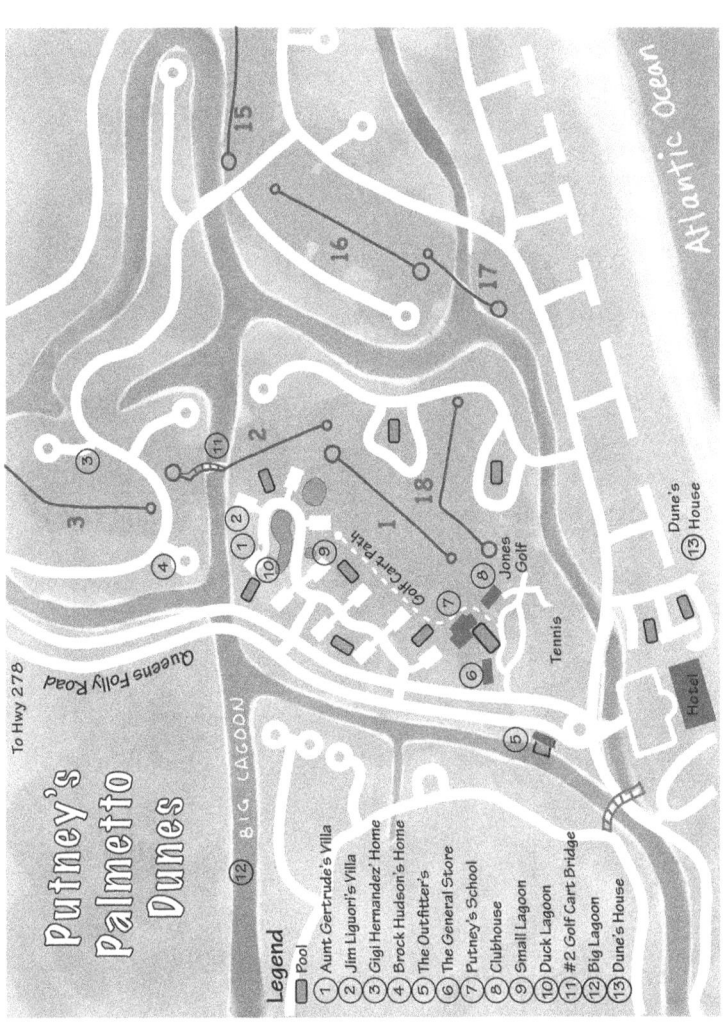

Chapter 1
Last Day of Freedom

"Hey Putney—you missed one!" calls my youngest brother, Archer, from around the corner of the deck.

"Really? Where?" I say, jumping up from painting Kodiak Trail Rocks. My favorite design so far is the salamander. They're like the small, bright green lizards you see everywhere here on Hilton Head Island.

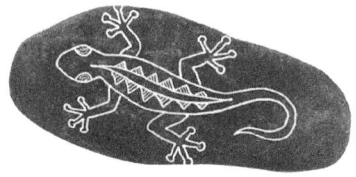

"There," he says, pointing to a large green caterpillar with black stripes and yellow dots, munching on a leaf of parsley. Archer is two years older than me. He has blond hair and hazel eyes, and lots of muscles from swimming and wrestling. This is the first year we'll be attending different schools, and it makes me sad. He's starting 9th grade. I'm starting 7th grade. Tomorrow.

"Thanks! Can you wait while I get a pair of scissors?"

I ask. Black swallowtail caterpillars, like many butterfly caterpillars, are designed to blend in with the leaves of the plants they eat. It's a survival tactic. It doesn't always work.

I've always loved butterflies. It's one of the best things about Hilton Head—lots of butterflies. I figure this is my chance to try my hand at rearing caterpillars. I want to see if I can observe the moments of metamorphosis—when a caterpillar turns into a chrysalis, and later when the butterfly emerges. I figure that's as close to magic as I'll get. As an aspiring artist/inventor, that is food for inspiration.

I grab a pair of scissors and a paper towel from the kitchen, then I carefully cut the stem of parsley below the caterpillar, as close to the ground as I can get.

"You're so weird, Putney. But in a good way," he teases me as I collect my prize.

INSIDE, AUNT GERTRUDE, technically *Great Great* Aunt Gertrude, asks about my latest caterpillar acquisition.

"Is it a Fred or a Ginger?" she asks, referring to my habit of naming my butterflies. We still watch old movies together. Just us girls. Some of my favorites have wonderful dance sequences in them, like anything with Fred Astaire and Ginger Rogers. He's the dancer who danced around all four sides of a room—floor, wall, ceiling, other wall, and floor again. One of his movies is Top Hat. So I think of him in a top hat and tuxedo with tails. When it came to thinking up names for my black swallowtail butterflies, I thought of him. Fred for the males, Ginger for the females.

"I don't know," I say, showing her my latest prize. "I only know how to tell the difference in the wing markings of the butterflies. Males have yellow spots on the edges of the wings. Females don't. They have smaller white spots, and a blue patch on their hind wings."

Curie, Aunt Gertrude's foxlike ruddy Somali cat, hops onto my shoulder from the bannister as I reach the stairs. Halfway up, Mom calls out to me, "Dinner will be ready in half an hour. And there's a package on your bed."

Chapter 2

The Package

I HEAD UPSTAIRS into the large irregular room that makes up the second floor of Aunt Gertrude's villa. Her condo was one of the large two bedroom / two bath plans all on one floor. It had a large attic area and pull-down stairs. An architect came up with plans to convert a part of the attic area to add a third bedroom and bath. Aunt Gertrude, like many other owners here in Queens Grant, added the third bedroom and bath years ago to get more space.

I open the door at the top of the stairs and turn right into the large bedroom area. My cubbyhole is off to the left, next to the bathroom. To the right is the main bedroom area. At the far end is a window with my "caterpillar tank" on a table.

As I reach the table, Curie hops off my shoulder and watches as I add my latest caterpillar to the others. Fortunately, the glass sides of the tank are too high for Curie to reach in and get to my caterpillars, so I let her watch.

I use small coke bottles filled with water as vases for the stems of parsley and butterfly weed. To keep the caterpillars from falling in the water, I cover the tops of the bottles with plastic wrap, secured with a rubber band. Then I poke a hole in the wrap just big enough for the stem. This keeps the leaves from drying out so fast, and keeps my caterpillars from accidentally drowning. At some point they will finish their munching and go "walkabout" to find a place to make their chrysalis or cocoon. No one is going to drown on my watch, not if I can help it.

I do a quick head count, and that's when I notice that *another* caterpillar has gone missing! Logan better not be using my caterpillars for fish bait! He was bragging about finding a new source the other day. I start to head downstairs to call him on it when I see the package on my bed. Well, air mattress, but it will do until we finally settle. If we settle.

The package is wrapped in brown craft paper with a green gauzy ribbon. No markings to tell where it came from. Then I notice a brown envelope tucked beneath the ribbon with my name on it. I pull it out and open the envelope. Inside is a card. I recognize the words on the front—it is one of my favorite quotes:

Just when the caterpillar thought the world was over, it became a butterfly.

There's only one person this could be from. I open the card and read the following:

"My dear Putney,

I have never taught another student with your unique gifts and passion for Science, Art, and Math. Pursue your passions and learn all you can. Do not fear failure, for we learn more from our failures than we do from our successes. Enclosed is a gift for you that you may find helpful on your journey.

May the road rise to meet you.
May the wind be always at your back.
May the sun shine warm upon your face,
the rains fall soft upon your fields and,
until we meet again,
may God hold you in
the palm of his hand.
– Miss Pepper"

I am speechless. I feel my eyes blur as I fight back tears. Dear Miss Pepper, my favorite teacher from Kodiak Elementary. She taught science, art, and math—a somewhat unusual combination. I had her for half of every day. How kind and thoughtful of her to think of me!

I pick up the package. It's rectangular, but soft around the edges, like it's wrapped in tissue paper. I pull off the bow and wind the ribbon into a roll. Then I tear into the brown craft wrapping paper. Inside is a layer of thick lime green tissue paper. I remove this layer to find… an iPad! It's beyond anything I could have wished for as a gift.

It's not in an Apple package though, so it may not be new. But I love it. I've always wanted one. It's already installed in a grey/black case. I plug it in to charge it and then press the home button to boot it. A logo displays on the screen while it's booting that is similar to, but isn't quite, the Apple logo. There's a circle with a bite out of it where the apple should be, and an arch over it instead of a leaf. Could that be an eye? There are smaller dots, in what I now guess to be the iris, that seem to rotate, like a progress wheel. The logo starts out grey on a black background, then flashes to a golden yellow, almost like my eye color. Then the screen background changes to aqua and the home screen comes up.

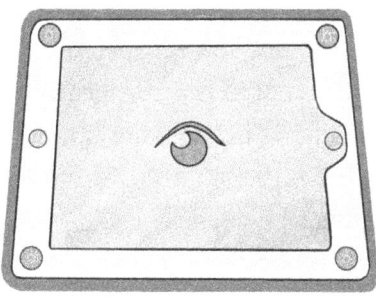

JUST THEN THE four bronze colored screw-like-things in the corners glow, their centers open to small pin pricks like a camera lens aperture. Four beams of golden light project to a pyramid point above the tablet and seem to scan my eye.

Startled, I drop the iPad and scuttle backwards like a crab until I hit the side of my air mattress.

Across the room, I hear Curie hiss, then the soft pads of her feet as she races towards me.

Now the iPad is flat on the floor, and the beams of light project to form a point about 12 inches above the iPad. A hologram figure appears. It's a bit of a Princess Leia moment. The figure that appears is not unlike Princess Leia in appearance, with dark brown hair in coiled braids on the sides of her head. This girl is clad in lime green instead of white and has glowing golden eyes. It reminds me of a hummingbird, hovering in mid-air. She looks at me silently, darting here and there above the iPad, as if to give me a careful once-over. The beams of light track her progress.

Next to me, Curie bats at the light, but her paws pass right through it.

"Who are you?" I finally whisper after a few heartbeats, which seem to last an eternity. What I really want to ask is "What are you?" but that seems too rude. I remind myself that this is a gift from Miss Pepper. Surely it can't be dangerous.

Finally, the green sprite of a girl speaks to me. "Hello, you must be Putney. I'm your virtual assistant. Like Siri, just a more advanced interface."

"What's your name?" I ask as my racing heartbeat steadies. "What kind of iPad is this?"

"Well, think of this as a very special advanced prototype iPad," she says, answering the second question first and drawing out the "i" in iPad.

The eye icon on the home screen winks at me, and

I gasp. It's a magic eye. This is a magic *eye*Pad, not iPad.

"You're a magic *eye*Pad," I guess. "*Eye* as in *eyeball*, not *i* as in *internet*."

"Yes!" the pixie beams at me.

Chapter 3
Sam

"What's your name? What should I call you?" I press, not to be deterred. This feels important. First contact and all that.

"Well, I could tell you, but there is magic in a name. The magic will be stronger if you can guess it on your own." The pixie darts about, sizing me up. She suddenly looks down at a point on the floor. I follow her gaze, expecting to see a "Palmetto bug" or a small lizard which seem to turn up unexpectedly here on Hilton Head, but all I see is the note from Miss Pepper on the floor.

Besides me, Curie stretches up on her hind legs to bat at the pixie. The pixie hovers, just out of Curie's reach, her eyes now focused back on me.

"What happens if I guess wrong?" I ask. I need to figure out the rules of this game. "Can you give me a hint?"

"Your favorite things in letters three, think of them and you'll see me," she blurs just then, darting around, the light beams leaving the after-image of the letter "S" on my retina.

S. Siri? But no, surely not Siri. That would be too easy. I glance down at the note from Miss Pepper, skimming it again, looking for a clue that begins with "S" when I come across the phrase, "…your unique gifts and passion for *S*cience, *A*rt, and *M*ath." And I have a *National Treasure* moment, the letters leaping off the page to form the name…

I gasp out loud as the revelation hits me. "Sam!"

"Well done, Putney!" Sam smiles broadly. "We're going to have such fun!"

"What can you do?" I ask. Suddenly a multitude of questions pop into my head. "What if someone sees you? Do you always appear as a hologram? Can I take you to school?"

"Hmm," ponders Sam, "there are rules of course, but there is magic in everything you say and do, so you never really know what you can do until you try. There's a lot of magic in seeking. The trick is often in asking the right questions."

"So you mean that I supply some of the magic by the questions I ask?"

"Think of it as a magical recharge cycle."

"What happens if someone sees you, as a hologram, flitting above the *eye*Pad screen?"

"The opposite of a magical recharge cycle, I expect," Sam speculates. "In fact, that's the key rule. You can't let an outsider prove the existence of magic. It would upset the balance of everything."

"So, I need you to use a different user interface when I use you in public," I say, imagining someone looking over my shoulder and causing a scene. I cannot let this happen. "Like a Siri voice interface?"

"That's certainly an option. But it's so overdone, and so limiting."

"But if you're tethered to the beams of light, what other options do we have that won't attract attention?"

"Well, you know, I'm not exactly sure until we try. But the magic feels very strong and I feel so free, I think I could break these tethers and move about without them. But you'll have to choose a physical form for me."

"How would that work? You take a physical form when I wake you up, then fade away when I put you to sleep?"

"Something like that. You could use the *eye*Pad anytime as a regular iPad without me, just like you can use an Apple iPad without Siri. You would call me specifically."

I look at Sam's brilliant lime green figure as it flits about over the *eye*Pad, and a memory stirs of a beautiful lime green lizard. The small lizards are everywhere on the island, in different shades of green and brown. I was wishing for one as a pet just the other day, but they are so shy of people.

"Sam, what are the small green lizards seen everywhere around this island? Can you pull up some information on them for me?"

"Excellent idea. Let's see what Wikipedia has to say," Sam says, smiling as she continues.

> *"The Carolina anole is an arboreal anole lizard native to the southeastern United States... It is also sometimes referred to as the American chameleon due to its ability to change color from several brown hues to bright green, and its somewhat similar appearance and diet preferences..."*

"And you see them everywhere; they even get into buildings. So no one would think anything of seeing a green anole with me. And the camouflage ability would be perfect!"

"Is that your choice?" Sam presses. "I need you to say the words, *Sam, I name thee green anole.*"

Just then I hear steps on the stairs. My cubbyhole is just on the other side of the door.

"Hurry," Sam whispers.

"Sam, I name thee green anole," I say in a low voice.

Several things happen at once. I hear a sudden "poof" and a hiss at the same time that the door bangs open. Sam disappears in a small puff of smoke as the beams of light are suddenly cut off. The apertures on the strange bronze screws close.

A split second later I hear a small thud as a small green anole hits the screen of my *eye*Pad. It scuttles over the edge and disappears. Curie pounces on the screen, then pokes her paws under the edge of the *eye*Pad where Sam disappeared, trying to catch her.

Chapter 4
An Interruption

WHAT HAVE I DONE? Have I freed her? Frantic about losing Sam, I flip the *eye*Pad over and notice a new design on the case. On the side bevel of the black case is a white line drawing of a green anole. Almost like the design I painted on one of my Kodiak Trail Rocks.

Curie bats her paws at the design. I quickly turn the *eye*Pad back over and set it on the ground as Dad enters the room.

"Hey Putt—here's another package for you—special delivery from Miss Kristin." He lets out a grunt as he sets it down on the ground next to my air mattress with a thunk. "What's in this one, rocks?"

"Well, yeah, Dad," I confess. "I can't just go to Jewel Beach anymore, so I needed to stock up. She wanted to get me a going-away present and asked me what I wanted. And I told her what I *really* wanted was more Jewel Beach rocks. She knows the kinds of rocks I like—the smooth flat-shaped ones, charcoal grey with occasional streaks of white."

Dad rolls his eyes, but he gets it. After all, we all

collected sea glass, rocks, and copper wire on Jewel Beach. Just no one else was as extreme about it as I was. Me and my rocks.

"What's that?" he asks, noticing the *eye*Pad for the first time.

"It's a gift from Miss Pepper," I reply. "Can you believe it? I would never have imagined such a gift in a million years—my very own tablet! It looks like an iPad, but it didn't come in an Apple box, so I'm not sure what all it can do. I was just starting to check it out."

"That *is* amazing! Miss Pepper knows you well, so I'm sure she has a few surprises for you. Maybe it has that Apple pencil you've been dreaming of, too," he says smiling. "So what are your plans for the Putney fund now that you don't have to save for an iPad Pro?"

Hmm. Was Dad in on it? Is that why he persuaded me to wait when I was thinking about buying an iPad earlier?

Raising three kids on a Coast Guard rescue swimmer's salary, Mom became a master-budgeter. Even with Dad a flight surgeon now, we've continued our thrifty ways. After all, there's still college to save for.

As we got older, Mom and Dad started giving us more responsibility and input. We each have a budget for the things we need. Some things Mom just goes ahead and buys for us. But, I can choose a lot of my clothes, and if I want an upgrade—like an iPad Pro instead of a basic iPad—I can wait until I've saved enough money to get what I really want. If I find a way to get what I need for less than the budgeted amount, I can save that too. I scored a couple of great finds at Goodwill—two pairs of capris for $5 that would have cost $75 each in a regular store.

I have, well *had*, two major savings projects: an iPad Pro and a dog. I figured I needed about a thousand dollars for each of those. Suddenly, my dream of having my very own dog looks a lot closer.

"I'm about half-way to my dog fund goal," I say.

"Be very sure about what you want, Putney." Dad reminds me. "A dog is a commitment of 10-15 years. It's not just about the money, it's also the time to care for it. Feed it, walk it, take it to the vet for checkups."

"I understand," I say. No impulse buys. That's why they set the bar so high. I have to demonstrate I'm committed.

"I'm not sure you do," Dad continues. "Ask yourself why you really want a dog. Is it to be popular and make friends?"

I stare down at the ground, thinking, trying to be honest with myself. A dog is unconditional love. It's the perfect friend. The friend you can take with you when you move. The friend that will never turn her back on you.

Dad seems to understand what is going through my head. He knows me and he still loves me. He has guessed my secret motivation. I hesitate, then look up to meet his eyes.

He smiles at me. "To have a friend, you have to be

a friend, Putney. You're so smart and creative. I love that about you. But, you could work on the people skills a bit. Try being a friend to others first. Try being a part of a team. Learn to put others first."

I look down again, staring at a point on the floor. Curie nudges me, then starts purring as I stroke her soft fur.

"It's a new start tomorrow. Dinner's in twenty minutes. I'm grilling hamburgers on the deck, but we'll be eating inside. Bring your iPad. Everyone will love to see what Miss Pepper got you," he says as he turns to head back down the stairs.

Chapter 5
The Magic eyePad

I TAKE A DEEP BREATH and let it out slowly. I've come crashing down to earth, the excitement of opening the eyePad now overshadowed by my secret shame. I have not been a good friend to others, or not as good as I could have been.

Curie nudges me again.

I hesitate, then reach out to the *eye*Pad to hold it. Curie pounces, reaching for the spot underneath, still searching for the lizard. Distracted, I brush my hand over the screen, not really focusing on it anymore. Instead, I imagine tomorrow, walking up the steps to the new school, and seeing a group of kids chatting excitedly to each other. How to break the ice? I always feel so awkward when meeting new kids, and I have a really hard time remembering names. It feels so overwhelming to me.

I sigh, then look back down at the *eye*Pad in my hand. Where has Sam has gone? Did I just imagine her? But Curie is batting her paws all over the *eye*Pad, now that it's off the floor. I turn it over in my hand and take a closer look at the new lizard design on the back. What does it mean?

The design makes me think of the M. C. Escher drawing, "Reptiles." Interlocking reptiles form a 2D pattern on a sheet of paper surrounded by an assortment of books and other objects. His reptiles look more like alligators than anoles, though. The cool thing about this drawing is that Escher's reptiles emerge from the flat 2D drawing to become live 3D reptiles that walk around before morphing back into the 2D design on the other side of the drawing. His drawings are so creative, he's one of my favorite artists. Here's a sketch I attempted of his drawing.

A sketch of MC Escher's "Reptiles"

CURIE BATS the back of the anole. I gasp as the lines glow briefly, then fade.

I set the *eye*Pad down and stroke the back of the anole, down the back ridge line, imagining it to be a 3D anole. This time the lines glow bright green, and Sam emerges. I feel my spirits rise as Sam runs across the back of the *eye*Pad.

I grab Curie before she can pounce. Twisting to my left, I grab a piece of the brown paper, crumple it into a ball, then toss it across the room for Curie. She chases after it, and bats it around the room like an ice hockey puck.

"Hey, Sam! I was so worried when you disappeared," the words rush out of my mouth in a breathy whisper. Mom, Dad, Archer, and Logan may be outside on the deck, but Aunt Gertrude is likely still in the villa. At 92, she doesn't do stairs anymore, but her hearing is still sharp as a bat's. At least, her selective hearing is. Don't ask me how. Most people her age have hearing aids.

Sam gives me a brief tour of the *eye*Pad's standard features. It has capability equivalent to an iPad Pro, and even has an Apple Pencil, which slides into a slot in the back case. I notice a diagram of a pencil on the back, on the opposite side to the anole design. I just have to run my finger down the pencil design and a secret compartment slides out that holds the pencil. A charger for the tablet and Apple-style ear buds are also included.

Dear Miss Pepper seems to have thought of everything. Software has been loaded, which includes the

Adobe Sketch and Fresco programs, Kindle, and Audible apps, iPhotos, iMovie, Clips (because of course, it's magic and has the best of everything) as well as a spreadsheet, word processing, and presentation program. If it weren't for the different logo, it would pass for an iPad. Of course it has built in internet access and cameras, and web storage for files. Just like a real iPad. Could the holographic assistant just be a super-advanced prototype? But no, I did not imagine Sam turning into a green anole and running around my room. That is magic. It *must* be.

I glance back at the four screw-type things in the corners. The ones that opened like an aperture when the beams of light appeared. Is there more to them than that?

Sam flicks her tail, getting my attention. "Tell me a little about yourself. What are your hobbies and dreams? What can I help you with?" she asks.

"Well, I like to paint and sew. Make things. Design my own versions of things, like my backpack and my mesh basket bags that I go tide-pooling with. I'd really like to be an artist/inventor like Leonardo da Vinci someday, but I have no idea how to go about that. I think Logan's going to be an engineer, he's so good at working on bikes. But I don't do anything like that," I say.

"Who said working on bikes was a requirement for becoming an inventor?" asks Sam.

"Well, it worked for the Wright Brothers. They

made the first successful human-powered flight," I say.

"True, but that's only one small area of innovation," says Sam.

"But sewing isn't anything like that," I say.

"Sewing is solving problems with fabric instead of metal and gears. It's a different medium, but it still offers design and problem-solving opportunities. Don't underestimate what you've already accomplished with your sewing. I bet there are lots of women engineers who grew up sewing as a hobby," replies Sam.

"Really?" I ask, becoming more hopeful.

"Of course," Sam replies. "Start with your hobbies and interests. That's where your passion will be. You are unique and special. You don't have to be anyone else to be an innovator. Design is a creative hobby, and creativity is like a muscle that gets stronger the more you work it."

"Wow, that's amazing. So, how should I start?" I ask.

"Well, since a picture is worth a thousand words, and sketches come in really handy in the design process, why don't I introduce you to one of my favorite drawing apps?" suggests Sam.

"That'd be great!" I say. I can already imagine myself drawing amazing sketches and plans for new inventions on my Magic *eye*Pad. After all, that's why I really wanted an iPad Pro.

Chapter 6

Dinner

"Hey, Putt—time for dinner!" my oldest brother, Logan, calls out to me. Three and a half years older than me, Logan is a really good athlete. He's been pulling advanced stunts on his bike since he could walk. He's tall, with blond hair and blue eyes. Like Archer, he makes friends easily. Another change in schools is no big deal to him.

I head downstairs, bringing my *eye*Pad to show everyone my gift from Miss Pepper.

"Miss Pepper?" Logan asks. "Was she the short teacher that always dressed in green?"

"Yes," I confirm.

"That's so cool!" says Archer. "She always did like you best. Wish I'd been her favorite."

Mom and Aunt Gertrude come to take a look. I show them the secret compartment for the Apple pencil. "I'll be able to do all my sketching and drawing on this now! I can't wait to start."

"That's a wonderful gift, Putney," Mom says, beaming. "I know it's what you've been saving for."

She squeezes my shoulder before heading back to the kitchen. "But put it down, it's time for dinner now," she says over her shoulder.

Dad comes inside, bringing a stack of grilled hamburgers, and we all take our places around the table. Aunt Gertrude says grace, then we pass the dishes. Bowls of three bean salad, German potato salad, and fresh fruit are passed around, and we all help ourselves. Dad dishes out the burgers. When everyone has been served, we dig in.

Conversation centers around the house-hunting process. We just moved here a couple weeks ago from Kodiak, Alaska, and have been staying with Aunt Gertrude in her villa on Hilton Head Island. Our stuff is still in a large shipping container somewhere between Kodiak and here.

It's between renting a house in Savannah near the air station where Dad works and buying a villa here on Hilton Head. A villa near the beach could be rented out to tourists next time we transfer, but it means less space for us now. Aunt Gertrude's villa is in a great location, only about a 15-minute walk to the beach in one direction, or to the shops in the other direction. And Hilton Head is very bike-friendly. I'd have lots of freedom and options here.

"If we buy here, space will be at a premium. We'll all be making a sacrifice to stay on Hilton Head, so give it some thought," says Dad. "I don't want to hear complaints and regrets later. Think this through. Once we commit, we will *all* need to make the best of it."

"You can stay with me as long as you need," offers Aunt Gertrude. She's told me that she would really like us to stay on Hilton Head. And so far, I really like it here. But the jury's out until I see what school is like. This won't be like Kodiak, where over half of us were "Coasties." There will be rich kids here. Lots of them. With my social skills, how will I possibly fit in?

On the other hand, I've never lived within walking distance of a swimmable beach before. Somehow, the streets of an average inland neighborhood seem boring by comparison. I love wandering on the beach and searching the tidal pools for hermit crabs, starfish, and sand dollars. Or watching dolphins swim by. I'd love to learn to paint ocean waves and clouds. I may never have another opportunity like this.

Besides, I'll get to be close to Aunt Gertrude as well as Aunt Mara when she and Uncle Leigh come down next week. They have a place in Queens Grant, too. Sometimes it feels like half of Cincinnati has moved down here.

AFTER DINNER, I clean up my paints, then head for a grassy patch by the lagoon where Sam coaches me through some drawing apps on the *eye*Pad. I pick a spot and start sketching the big lagoon, with palm trees and saw palmettos—a shrubby version of a palm tree. I snap pictures of a few birds. I'm definitely going to have to learn their names.

After about an hour of sketching, Sam tells me to take a break and shows me her *Virtual Reality* mode. "Imagine yourself as anything," Sam instructs. Thinking about my caterpillars, I imagine myself as a monarch butterfly, emerging from my chrysalis, expanding my wings and taking my first flight, soaring above the lagoon. It's amazing. I can feel the warmth of the sun and the wind beneath my wings as I take turns flapping and then gliding, while the sweet smell of nectar rises from the flowers below.

Before I know it, Mom calls me to get ready for bed, pulling me from the sky as a butterfly and dropping me back in reality–reality as a soon-to-be-new-student. Again. The anxiety of tomorrow returns, but now I have a secret friend. A little bubble of courage takes hold in me. I smile as I head upstairs and find a place for Sam on the end table by my air mattress.

Curie races into the room behind me, watching the *eye*Pad and Sam intently. Sam gives Curie a long look, then jumps down onto the floor.

"You're volunteering for the role of cat toy?" I ask.

"I always liked cats," says Sam. "Curie's a sweetie. We just need to get to know each other. Besides, I have some awesome tricks up my sleeves." At that moment, Curie pounces and Sam disappears right from under her feet, just to reappear on her shoulders. This starts the game of bucking bronco, with Curie spinning to the left almost like she's chasing her tail. But Sam has four legs with strong gripping toes on each. Sam giggles and nudges Curie behind the shoulders with her head. Curie rolls over and Sam disappears again, only to reappear just in front of her.

I wonder if Curie will actually let Sam ride her if I give her something else to chase, so I fish out the crumpled piece of brown craft paper and toss it onto the floor. Curie chases after it, and Sam jumps onto Curie's shoulders again. Curie repeats her stiff-legged stalker prance before pouncing on the paper ball, Sam riding securely on her shoulders, whooping with delight.

I watch for another ten minutes, until the game finally slows down. Curie rolls on her back and allows Sam to nudge her behind the ears. I switch the lights off, then pat my pillow, inviting Curie to join me on my bed. Sam finds her way to the *eye*Pad. I drift off to sleep with Curie purring in my ear and softly kneading my hair on the pillow.

Chapter 7
Dreams

BEING A BUTTERFLY is a really weird feeling. It's not like being a bird or a swimmer. My wings form a kind of stiff but flexible cape that's attached to my chest. There's a slit down the middle where my hind wings meet. I can seal it tight, but I can also move my body to either side of it. I use one set of muscles to pull my wings behind me and another opposing set to extend them. They actually attach to the inside of my chest cavity, the thorax, and I work the wings by contracting opposite sides of this cavity. Who knew?

Unlike birds, my arms are not wings. They're legs. I chose to be a monarch, so I only have four legs instead of six. More aerodynamic. We monarchs are long-distance fliers.

I learn to use a sort of swinging motion to hover in mid-air before landing on a flower to suck up a tasty drink. After so much flying, I'm hungry and thirsty. My legs extend to catch the flower head. It's a soft landing. It's funny, but I can taste with my feet. My mouth watering, I uncoil my long straw-like tongue thing. I think it's called a proboscis. It's kind of like an elephant's trunk, just a lot smaller. I take a long sip of tasty nectar. Mmm. That hits the spot.

"Nice landing, Putney!"

I jolt awake at the words in my head. In a split second, I come crashing back to earth, changing from a graceful butterfly to a clumsy human girl. I flail to catch myself before flying over the side of the bed, grabbing the quilt to stop my fall. Just when I think I've succeeded, the quilt slides, depositing me in a tangle of bedding on the floor. Curie looks down at me from the bed.

"Good morning, Putney," says Sam. "You have an interesting way of waking up. Archer and Logan were very boring and conventional by comparison. They're already downstairs. I think I'm going to have a lot of fun with you."

"Good morning, Sam! You weren't a dream!" I answer as I disentangle myself from the quilt. "What time is it?"

"You've got about half an hour for breakfast before you need to leave for school," she replies. "Archer and Logan have been up for an hour, but I heard your mom say she wanted to let you sleep in a bit longer."

I brush my teeth and brush my hair, then pull on the clothes I set aside to wear today. I check myself in the mirror. White t-shirt, peach capris—a real find at Goodwill—and white sneakers, basic and practical. I should be able to slide under the radar with that.

I need to do something with my long, light brown hair though, or the heat and humidity will kill me. I bend over, brushing my hair into a high ponytail and secure it with an elastic band. Now I look like I have a bush growing out of my head. Sighing, I start braiding it, securing the end with another elastic band. I won't win any style awards, but I won't be sweating too much either.

Sam gives an approving nod. "You look nice. Time for breakfast. I think I hear your mother calling."

"Okay, let's go," I say. Sam hops onto the *eye*Pad as I pick it up. I put it in my backpack, not quite closing the compartment, and we head down the stairs.

THE SMELL of bacon frying hits me as I come down the stairs. I hear the front door bang, then the chatter of Logan and Dad talking as they come in, back from a run on the beach I'm guessing. Aunt Gertrude sets the table. Archer heads in from the deck, and we all gather round the table.

Aunt Gertrude sits at the head of the table and says grace. Then we all dig in.

Chatter soon turns to the house-hunting process.

"What are you going to look at today?" Aunt Gertrude asks.

"We're looking at some single-family homes in Savannah," replies Mom.

"All of them have three or four bedrooms plus an office that could be converted into a bedroom, plus a two-car garage," Dad explains. "So you could each have your own bedroom."

AFTER BREAKFAST, I help clear dishes while Logan rushes upstairs for a quick shower after his run. Mom finishes packing lunches, then calls out to Logan and Archer to hurry up. She gives them each a quick hug as she ushers them out the door to catch the school bus.

I'm at a new school, a kind of temporary overflow site for 6th through 8th graders. It's just down the street, around the corner from the General Store. About a 5-minute bike ride or a 10-minute walk from here.

"You sure you don't want me to drive you on your first day?" Mom asks.

"No, Mom. I'll be fine. I have my registration letter and I know where it is. It's only a 5-minute bike ride from here," I say, trying to sound braver than I feel. "We go right past it every time we go to the beach."

Mom pulls me into a tight hug. "Have a wonderful day. I think this is going to be a very special school," she says, smiling down at me.

Dad comes up behind us, giving us both a hug. "Go get 'em, tiger," he says. "New day, new friends."

I hug them back, put my lunch in my backpack, and head out the door.

Chapter 8
Gigi

My school occupies a site that used to be rented to a lifestyle fitness gym, around the corner from the General Store and just to the left of the Robert Trent Jones Golf Course Club House. It's only about a 3-minute walk from here to the beach.

A middle-aged woman sitting at a table outside checks me in and hands me my schedule and locker assignment. A tent card reads, "Mrs. Roberts, Counsellor."

"Welcome, dear. I'm sure you'll love it here." Mrs. Roberts smiles at me. "Mr. DiPilla will be your homeroom teacher. Go inside the double doors, straight back into the hallway. It's the first room on your right."

I thank her, then enter the building, round the corner into the classroom indicated and immediately feel my face light up in a smile. There are real blackboards on the wall and two-person workstations with black chem-lab type countertops. This must be a science classroom. I love the feel of chalk on real slate blackboards, and the smooth black countertops.

Windows line the right side of the room, with a view of the golf driving range.

"Hello and welcome! You must be Putney Hicks. I'm your homeroom and science teacher, Mr. DiPilla."

I turn to the front of the classroom and see a round, short man, balding with a fringe of brown hair. He has kind eyes, and his smile lights up the room. He's wearing dark brown pants and shoes, with a white short-sleeved shirt and a rich greenish-brown bow tie that somehow brings out sparkles in his hazel eyes. He seems somehow ageless, neither old nor young.

"Yes, I am," I say. "How did you know?"

"Here, let me show you to your desk. You'll be sharing a lab table with Gigi Hernandez," he says, pointing. "That's Gigi over there, with the long brown hair."

I follow his gaze and see a girl with chestnut brown hair pulled back in a long braid with bangs framing her face chatting with a blonde girl in capris like mine, except they're a bit pinker.

A tall boy with blond hair enters the room from the other door, and the blonde girl calls out, "Bryce, how are you?" and heads over to him. The brunette laughs, then looking in my direction, makes her way over to the lab table.

"Hi! I'm Gigi Hernandez. What's your name? Are you new to South Carolina? Where do you live? What do you like to do?"

I laugh at the barrage of questions and start to

answer. "I'm Putney Hicks, and my family just moved here from Kodiak, Alaska. We're staying with my Aunt Gertrude, just up the road in Queens Grant, while we look for a place of our own."

"Queens Grant!" exclaims Gigi. "I'm not far from there by water, a bit further by road, unless you cut over the golf cart path from the second hole of the Robert Trent Jones course. Have you met Jim Liguori and Josh Teague? They live in Queens Grant, too. It's a nice location, so close to the beach and the General Store, and close enough to Shelter Cove to walk there too."

"No, we only arrived a couple weeks ago," I explain. "We drove from Alaska, and it took over three weeks. Our furniture hasn't arrived yet, which is okay since we don't have a house yet. But I'm short on clothes. Not that my Alaska clothes would help me much in this weather anyway. It barely gets above 60 in the summer there."

"That's practically winter here," laughs Gigi.

Two boys enter the room, deep in conversation, as they push through the door. The first has short brown wavy hair, brown eyes, and the tanned skin that comes from spending a lot of time outdoors in the sun. He is followed by a short thin boy with blond hair and sparkling blue eyes.

"Hey Jim, hey Josh—how was your summer?" Gigi calls over to them. "Hey, I want to introduce you to someone."

The two boys say hello and join us at the lab table.

Gigi makes the introductions.

"Putney, this is Jim Liguori and Josh Teague. Jim's a budding naturalist. He knows all the birds, their names and habits around the lagoons. His parents own the Outfitters store, and he helps with lagoon tours and managing all the equipment—canoes, kayaks, paddle boards and such. His family lives in Queens Grant near the big lagoon, not far from the golf cart bridge by the second hole.

"Josh here can do magic with videos. He's got a real knack for special effects and editing. He's a natural storyteller. His family lives in Queens Grant, too, in the building closest to the beach," Gigi continues.

"And this is Putney Hicks, from Alaska. She's staying with her Aunt Gertrude in Queens Grant for the time being," Gigi finishes.

Jim's eyes narrow as if in concentration, then his expression clears. "Would that be Miss Goering?" Jim asks. "She's a real pistol. Lives off the big green field in the Kensington cluster. She always has a story to tell us and a plate of amazing pastries she calls Kipfels at holidays."

"That's my Aunt Gertrude," I laugh. "Technically, she's my Great Great Aunt. She's had an amazing life, worked at Wright Aerospace as a secretary. She knows so much about the aircraft engine business, and she's traveled so much, she always has interesting stories to tell."

"Well, I'm just down the other end of the green from you. Hey, you'll have to come with us canoeing some time. There's a place to enter the lagoon just down from Miss Goering's deck that we use. My sister Jenn and I often go out on the big lagoon after dinner."

The homeroom bell rings and Mr. DiPilla urges us to take our seats.

Maybe this new school won't be so bad after all.

Chapter 9

Science Class

AS IT TURNS OUT, science is my first class of the day. Mr. DiPilla kicks off class with a question and a magic trick, "What's heavier, air or water?"

Several hands pop up and the girl with blonde hair and capris like mine answers, "Water of course, because it sinks to the ground."

Mr. DiPilla seems pleased by this response. He illustrates his next question by taking a beaker of water and an ordinary drinking straw and asks, "If water is heavier than air, how can I lift a column of water with a straw and nothing but air underneath to hold it up?" He demonstrates this by putting the straw into the beaker of water until the straw is half filled with water. Then, placing his finger over the top of the straw, he lifts it out of the beaker. The water does not leak out.

This time there are no volunteers. "Anyone care to take a guess?" asks Mr. DiPilla.

After a pause, Mr. DiPilla takes out a ball and holds it up. "What will happen to this tennis ball if I drop it?"

"It will fall to the ground," replies Jim.

"Very good," says Mr. DiPilla. "Do you know why?"

"Gravity," puts in another boy with light brown hair and hazel eyes.

"Excellent, Brock," says Mr. DiPilla. "So, when I hold the ball, I'm resisting the force of gravity on the ball which is equal to the ball's weight."

Several heads nod at this. We've heard of gravity.

"Anyone care to guess what is resisting the weight of the water in the straw?" Mr. DiPilla asks. He waits a few seconds, then turns to me, "Putney, care to take a crack at this?"

I look up to see Mr. DiPilla smiling at me. For some reason, he thinks I can answer this question.

Out of the corners of my eyes, I see that most of the other students are watching me. I glance down briefly to gather my thoughts, then glance around the room, stalling for time. Most of the students shift in their seats and look away as I glance in their direction. The blond boy, Bryce, I think, smirks at me. He is enjoying this. Next to me, Gigi smiles her support. Across the room, a boy with the light brown hair and hazel eyes—Brock?—returns my gaze. I feel my cheeks burn and look away. Behind me I hear muffled whispers. As I turn my head, I see a trio of blonde girls stare at me as they whisper among themselves. Ponytail girl looks away, but the girl with short curly hair continues to whisper into the ear of the girl with capris like mine. Capri-girl lifts her chin and returns my gaze, the left side of her mouth curving into a smile of superiority. An unspoken gauntlet has been thrown down. She does not think I can answer this question.

Something clicks inside me. I can do this. I *will* do this, I tell myself, and I find that I do have a clue. I think back to my scuba training and remember a random fact… it takes 33 feet of water to equal one atmosphere of pressure.

I have a choice now. I can be the super-smart-new-freak in town, or the invisible hasn't-got-a-clue new girl. For better or worse, I decide just to be me. So I square my shoulders and take a deep breath as I return my gaze to the straw. I twist my hands, take one last second to organize my thoughts and then start.

"Air is all around us, pressing against everything—every surface. It takes the weight of 33 feet of water to equal one atmosphere of air pressure. So I guess when you put your finger on the top of the straw, you cut off the air pressure pushing down on the water in the straw. So you only have air at the bottom pushing up? And the water in the straw is only a few inches tall, nowhere close to 33 feet high, so it isn't heavy enough to overcome the air pressure holding it in?"

"That's a good description," smiles Mr. DiPilla. "So what will happen if I take my finger off the top of the straw?"

"Um… Now you have air pressure pushing down on the water as well as pushing up? So they cancel out?

And the weight of the water is heavier than air, so it falls to the ground," I say, guessing.

Mr. DiPilla beams at me, and then demonstrates. The water runs out of the straw, of course. There are still several puzzled looks, as everyone tries to understand what happened. Mr. DiPilla continues his carefully crafted lesson on volume, weight, density, and force balances.

And he uses math to explain it all. This is my kind of teacher. Magic trick, science, and math. I actually learn something and have fun doing it.

THE BELL RINGS and it's time to head to art class. As I rise, Gigi asks me how I knew all that stuff about atmospheric pressure. As I start to explain, I overhear capri-girl saying, "What a freak… yellow eyes and those capris are so last year. I used to have a pair just like them, but I donated them to Goodwill. No one would be caught dead in peach this year."

Gigi seems to overhear the comment too because she adds, "You have really pretty eyes. I've never seen golden eyes like yours before, not really hazel or green or brown, but much lighter. Is there a name for that eye color?"

"Amber," I reply, grateful for the compliment. Today I am branded a freak yet again, but I also seem to have found a friend. And perhaps made an enemy.

Chapter 10
Art Class

THE ART CLASSROOM is at the end of the main hall on the left. Windows overlook a landscaped courtyard and pool. Inside is a tall lanky man, with short brown hair, smiling brown eyes and a close-cropped beard. He wears a short-sleeved shirt, but no tie.

Mr. Shelley introduces himself and passes out a supplies list. Besides the usual sketch pad, art pencils, and eraser is an unusual item–a sit-upon.

"What's a sit-upon and why do we need one?" inquires the girl with capris like mine.

"It's something to sit upon," replies Mr. Shelley. "We'll be sketching outside several days a week, learning from the greatest master of all–nature. So, we'll need to be very portable as a result. A sit-upon will protect you from damp grass or sand while you sketch."

"Do you have a recommended product we should buy?" asks another girl with blonde hair, pulled back in a ponytail.

"Consider this an opportunity to unleash your

creativity on your first design project," counters Mr. Shelley. "In fact, let me challenge you to come up with something using only materials you have on hand at home for your first attempt."

"You mean we have to make something? *Sew*?" asks capri-girl with disdain. You'd think sewing was a disease, like leprosy or something.

"I want you to open your minds up and consider what you *need* in a sit-upon, and then look around your home to figure out what you already have that you could use to *MacGyver* a solution," clarifies Mr. Shelley. "At a minimum, a garbage bag and some newspaper will do. Everyone should be able to manage that easily enough."

"When do we need to have this?" asks a girl with freckles and dark curly hair.

"Weather permitting, we start sketching in the field tomorrow. Look on this as an opportunity to test your design skills. Try to quickly come up with a minimum viable product–MVP. Doesn't have to be fancy, just functional. Then you'll learn what works and what doesn't, and you can roll improvements into your next design. That's called rapid prototyping—you can google it."

"How will we be graded on this?" asks a girl with short curly blonde hair.

"You'll grade yourself when you use it. You are your own customer, not me."

"But the best design will have bragging rights," pops

up another girl, with mocha skin and exquisite braids.

"Unofficial bragging rights," agrees Mr. Shelley with a laugh. "Maybe we'll even take a class vote and make it official. Okay? Enough said. Let me introduce you to Zentangles."

With that, he introduces us to the concept of a Zentangle, which is basically structured doodling. It gives you an opportunity to work with different line patterns and shading, and the repetitive nature of the design is calming. I find it to be fun.

At the end of class, everyone's look different, but similar. We've all put our own stamp on the design somehow. Here's my first Zentangle. I love the patterns, and they give me new ideas for my rocks.

As the bell rings at the end of class, Mr. Shelley reminds us, "Don't forget, you're first version of a sit-upon doesn't have to be perfect. You'll do a better job with your design if you actually try something first. Then you'll know what you like and don't like about it, and what you wish it had that it doesn't."

OUTSIDE IN THE HALLWAY, capri-girl walks just in front of me. I hear her complain to ponytail-girl and the curly blonde, saying, "What a waste of time. Wish I could drop art class. What good is it anyway? Everyone knows the real money's in STEM or professional athletics. Who cares about making a sit-upon?"

"What about Leonardo da Vinci?" I say, butting my nose in. "He was an artist, inventor, and engineer. And we're learning design. That's useful."

Capri-girl stops, turns around, looks me up and down once and replies, "Who asked you? Anyway, I'll be earning millions of dollars, while I bet you end up working at Walmart for minimum wage to pay for your art supplies."

With that, she turns on her heels and walks away, her two blonde minions in tow.

Well, we aren't going to be best friends anytime soon. She must be one of the uber-rich kids I was worried about fitting in with. But who'd want to be friends with a snob like that anyway? I shrug it off and head to math class.

THE REST of the morning passes quickly. Math builds on the science lesson, giving the "recipe" or formula for density. It's not quite Algebra, but it's laying the foundation for it. One thing about being the youngest in a family of three siblings, you get introduced to advanced math topics. Dad has this trick of getting Logan and Archer to study for a test by "teaching" a lesson to someone—usually me as the youngest. He says there is nothing like the exercise of "teaching" a subject to someone else to really learn it. But I never get to be the teacher for Logan or Archer. My turn is always to come "tomorrow." Only Mom or Dad will sit with me to help me prep for a test.

Chapter 11
Lunch

AT LUNCH, Gigi invites me to sit with her and some of her friends. I am one of only a few students to pack a lunch. Margot French, the girl with freckles and curly dark hair is another. JZ Sparrow, the girl with the mocha complexion and exquisite braids joins us. In a whisper, I ask who the blonde girl with the snide remarks is.

"Oh, that's Sue Wexford. She's really good at tennis—she's won some junior tournaments. They're hoping she'll make it to the U. S. Open some day," replies Gigi.

"She and her best friend, Lynne Smythe-Dixon—that's the girl with really short curly blonde hair—live on the same street in Leamington," Margot adds. "That's the most prestigious and exclusive part of Palmetto Dunes. My mom owns her own cleaning business, and they are two of her clients. Sue's mom is a big realtor on the island, and her dad is a famous surgeon. I think his specialty is knee surgery. Her other friend, Liz Ogelthorpe—the girl with the ponytail, lives in a house on the beach just down from Dunes House. So, super-rich, too. They're almost inseparable."

"Wow… you mean we're going to school with the next Venus Williams?" I ask, showing off my limited tennis savvy. Noticing the odd look from JZ, I continue, "Look, I know Serena has been more successful, but Venus was first. It's always hardest when you don't know whether something is possible, than when you have a role model showing you it *is*."

"Can you say that again in English?" teases JZ.

"My brother Logan is oldest. He struggled with some subjects in school. When Archer came along, he cruised through those same subjects. When I had to learn the multiplication tables, I spent about two minutes worrying about whether I could memorize them before I stopped myself. I figured if Logan and Archer could do it, then I could. Maybe it didn't make it any more fun, but at least I didn't waste my time worrying. I gritted my teeth and got to work," I explain.

"You say the strangest things," laughs JZ. "Well, it's way too early to tell. But Venus was never spoiled the way Sue is. I don't think Sue has the grit it takes to make it in the majors."

"Well, she does work really hard, and she has every other material advantage," says Gigi. "Plus, she's really smart. If tennis doesn't work out for her she could go into almost any other career."

I start to get up to take my trash to the garbage

can, when Margot suddenly coughs and asks me where I'm living on the island.

I spin around to answer her when my foot hits something slick and slides out from underneath me. I careen backwards, my arms flailing wildly, and I crash backwards into… not a person, but a lunch tray. I hear a crash and land on the floor next to an assortment of silverware, napkins, an apple, and a bottle of milk. Somehow my unintentional victim managed to hang onto the tray and the rest of the food.

"What kind of klutz are you?" a voice snipes from above me. "Can't you watch where you're going?"

I start apologizing immediately. As I turn around, I look up in horror to see Sue Wexford standing there, with the remains of a plateful of lasagna splattered across her silk shirt.

Gigi springs up immediately, helping Sue with the worst of the mess. "Hey Sue, let me help you with that. Have you met Putney? She just moved here from Alaska."

"I'm so sorry. My foot slid right out from underneath me," I say, scrambling to get up, but sliding on the slick spot again.

Sue turns and literally looks down her nose at me. She seems to notice me for the first time, and stares hard at the leg of my capris. "You must tell me where you buy your clothes," she says with a crocodile smile.

WE ARE WEARING IDENTICAL CAPRIS, right down to the embroidered design at the bottom of the right leg.

The only difference is that hers are a slightly pinker shade than mine. Watermelon perhaps? I feel my cheeks burn as I try to think what to say, and what the consequences will be. "Um… I don't remember," I lie. Sometimes I can get by with saying GW's, but my gut is telling me Sue is out for blood. If I give her a thread to pull on, she will keep pulling until she unravels the entire sweater, and I am left naked and ashamed. So I go on the offensive instead. Looking around frantically for an idea to bail me out, I notice a beautiful gold necklace hanging near her throat.

"Wow, that's a cool necklace," I say, grasping at straws. But it truly is a unique design. "I've never seen a design like that. It seems like something from a petroglyph or something. Does it have a special meaning?"

"It's an original design from St. John, inspired by the rock carvings there, made of solid gold. It's worth $1000 and was a present from my father for winning a Juniors Ladies Cup tournament in March," huffs Sue as two blonde girls—Lynne and Liz—hurry to her side. She hands one girl her tray, while the other ushers her towards the restroom to clean up.

My heart is still racing and I can feel the flush of heat on my cheeks as Margot helps me pick up the things strewn across the floor, then helps me to my feet.

"Are you okay?" asks Gigi. "That looked like a hard fall."

"Well, you certainly made an impact on Sue," chuckles JZ.

"Yeah, a very unique, red impact," joins in Margot. "I don't think it's quite the right shade to match her capris though."

"I am so embarrassed. How will I ever live this down?" I groan.

How do I get myself into these situations? Why can't I be more graceful?

Chapter 12

Assembly

THE AFTERNOON passes in a blur, and before I know it I'm entering the "Multi-Purpose Room" for a General Assembly during 6th period. Tables line the walls, staffed with teachers. Principal Hauck stands at the end of the Multi-Purpose Room behind a podium and waits for us to settle on the floor. Gigi, Margot, JZ, and I find an open spot together near one of the tables on the side with the floor-to-ceiling windows. We have a nice view of the courtyard and pool.

"Welcome to Palmetto Dunes Middle School," Principal Hauck begins. "We are kicking off a pilot program this year. We have a new STEAM initiative, which stands for science, technology, engineering, art, and math. Our first event will be a science fair/art exhibit to be held this Friday. You are encouraged to enter one event. Your science and art teachers have more information for you at the tables to my right, along with entry categories and set-up times.

"There is one other unique activity planned. Since we have a pool, and Mr. McCabe has obtained donations of equipment for student use, we will be offering underwater hockey during gym period through September. Alternately, students can choose to enroll in one of the tennis or golf lesson programs offered just across the street.

"Underwater hockey is played around the world but is especially popular in the United Kingdom, Australia, New Zealand, and South Africa, where it's often played in school. Although it isn't an Olympic sport, there are world championships. It's been gaining ground in the U.S. over the past couple decades, and more schools are starting programs. Charleston has a big club, and last year a club was started at the Island Rec Center for all ages."

I gasp at the mention of underwater hockey. Already I can imagine myself zooming along underwater like a dolphin. Sounds like my kind of sport. Gigi giggles next to me. "Is that for real?" she asks.

Jim Liguori, sitting right behind us with Josh Teague, overhears and answers, "I started playing last year, and it's a lot of fun—if you're adventurous enough to put your head underwater and dive to the bottom of the pool. That's where the game is played—on the pool bottom."

Principal Hauck dismisses us and encourages us to look at the tables, which include information about upcoming field trips as well as after-school activities and the science fair/art exhibit.

The tables for the science fair/art exhibit are right next to us, so we start there. We giggle as we chatter, running from table to table, gathering forms and information about each activity, talking about the things we like to do in our spare time. We talk about hiking and painting, and surfing in the ocean.

I pull out one of my Kodiak Trail Rocks and explain how people design them and hide them on trails for others to find. JZ thinks they're really cool. Gigi tells me I should show them to Miss Tempura at Sheik Boutique. "She's always looking for unique items to offer, and features local artists," she adds. "Maybe we can bike down after school tomorrow and I can introduce you."

I feel a smile lighting up my face. "That would be so cool! Do you really think she'd be interested?"

The four of us make plans to bike to Coligny Plaza after school tomorrow.

Then the bell rings at 2:45 signaling that school is dismissed. I run to my locker, gather up my books and backpack, and head outside to grab my bike. You'd think it'd be steamy hot here in August, but so much of the island has large live oaks and sea pines, that most of the bike paths have shade much of the day. There are a few, like the golf cart path, that only have sea pines on one side. That one gets morning sun but has shade in the afternoon, during the hottest part of the day. I just have to learn the shade patterns and adjust my route to pick the best one for the time of day.

Chapter 13
Aunt Gertrude

AUNT GERTRUDE greets me as I enter the villa, first one back. Mom and Dad are still out looking at rental properties in Savannah. Out of the corner of my eye, I see Sam escaping from my backpack as I set it down under the foyer table.

"How was school?" she asks.

My words come tumbling out in a rush as I explain my humiliation at knocking the tray of food into Sue Wexford.

"Aside from that, tell me about the good parts," she prompts. Aunt Gertrude is always quick to put things in balance. "Did you make some new friends?"

"I met this really cool girl, Gigi. She's kind of like the impossible girl on Dr. Who. At least I think of her as the impossible girl."

"What makes her so amazing?" inquires Aunt Gertrude.

"She seems to genuinely like everybody and see the best in them. Even this geeky kid that is really good with A/V. You can't help but like her. Even Sue

Wexford treats her with respect. JZ and Margot are really cool, too. We're going to Sheik Boutique after school tomorrow. Gigi thinks Miss Tempura might sell my trail rocks in her boutique."

"What were classes like?"

"Science and art are my favorites so far. I'm so excited—I've got my first design project. I never thought I'd learn to be an inventor in art class. And we've got a science fair/art exhibit this Friday. So I need to come up with projects for that."

"Your mother said you can go swimming for an hour before dinner, but to start on your homework when you get home. Dinner's planned for 6:00 p.m."

"Okay. Design project first, I think. Do you have a tape measure?" I ask.

"Here you go," says Aunt Gertrude, as she pulls a tape measure out of the kitchen drawer. "Let me know if there's anything else you need."

I pick up my *eye*Pad and head out onto the deck, Sam scurrying behind. Perfect! Some one-on-one time with Sam before my brothers explode onto the scene.

Chapter 14
The Sit-Upon Design Project

I SIT DOWN at the patio table under the big green umbrella, facing out toward the big lagoon. Two kayakers glide noiselessly by. Sam pops out of my backpack.

"Okay—sit-upon design project first," I say to Sam. "I need a water-resistant cover and some sort of padding and handle. I'd also like a pocket to hold my sketch pad. But what size should I make it?"

"An easy way to test options is just to grab some things and test them," says Sam. "That's called rapid prototyping, like Mr. Shelley mentioned. You work quickly to get a minimum viable product (or MVP). Then you use it to see how well it works to refine your design."

I head back inside and score some bubble wrap and an IKEA bag, which measures about 24 inches wide by 20 inches high. I lay it on the deck. It's big enough for me to sit cross-legged on it. I like that.

Next, I roll out some of the pink bubble wrap. It's nearly the exact width of the IKEA bag, and I can fold it to make several layers. I really don't want to use something that's going to pop underneath me, but it would be lightweight and waterproof if it works. Nothing's lighter than air. Well, except for helium. That doesn't count.

I fold the bubble wrap into four layers, then carefully sit down upon it. No popping.

Encouraged, I stand up and plop down on it with more force. Still no popping. This will work!

"Great work, Putney!" encourages Sam. "You've got your first prototype. Now let's go for a walk and test it on grass and concrete."

We test it out, then Sam has me sketch out the design on the *eye*Pad. I use layers like she showed me yesterday to organize my sketch elements so I can copy parts that I like and tweak them easily. Here are the notes I wrote down about it. I put a plus (+) in front for good things, and a minus (–) for bad things.

SIT-UPON PROTOTYPE #1 – IKEA bag with bubble-wrap padding
- \+ Light
- \+ Big enough to sit on cross-legged—GREAT! (This will be very nice if sitting on the sand!)
- \+ Can carry sketchpad
- – HUGE (at 24" wide by 20" high, it's almost 1/3 of my height!)
- – Shoulder straps fall down too easily

Wish List:
- Would like separate pocket for sketch pad
- Would like cross-body shoulder strap option
- Would like smaller size to carry... fold down?

Here's my sketch of what this looked like. This was just a very quick rough sketch to show size relative to me and how I'd use it.

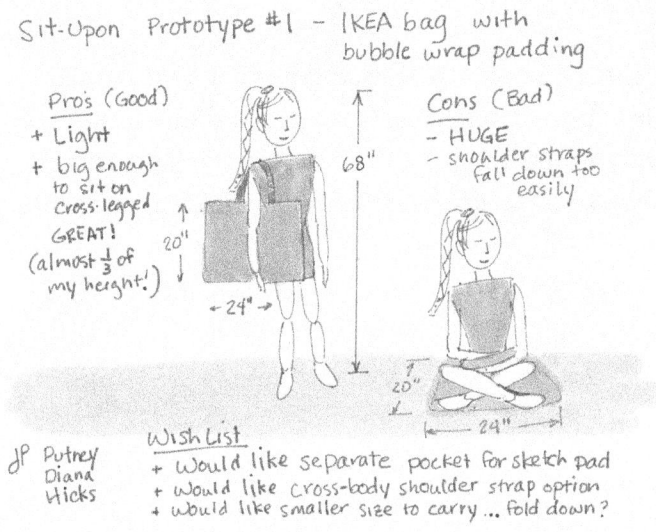

"GREAT WORK! We've learned a lot very quickly. What do you want to try next?" asks Sam.

"Well, the grass was pretty soft, and the concrete wasn't that bad to sit on. Maybe just a tarp would work? And I could fold it down to any size." I say.

I take the padding out of the IKEA bag and test it to see how it would feel to sit on without any padding. Here's the results of my second prototype test:

SIT-UPON PROTOTYPE #2–Tarp without Padding
- \+ Very light!
- \+ Can fold up—compact
- \+ Could make large enough to spread out on!!
- \- Not as comfortable on concrete

<u>Wish List</u>:
- Would need separate tote bag to carry this and my sketchpad and pencils.

HERE'S my sketch of Prototype #2. I don't have anything defined to carry it yet, so I didn't show a tote with me standing. That's a separate problem. Although I guess I could just use the empty IKEA bag on its own.

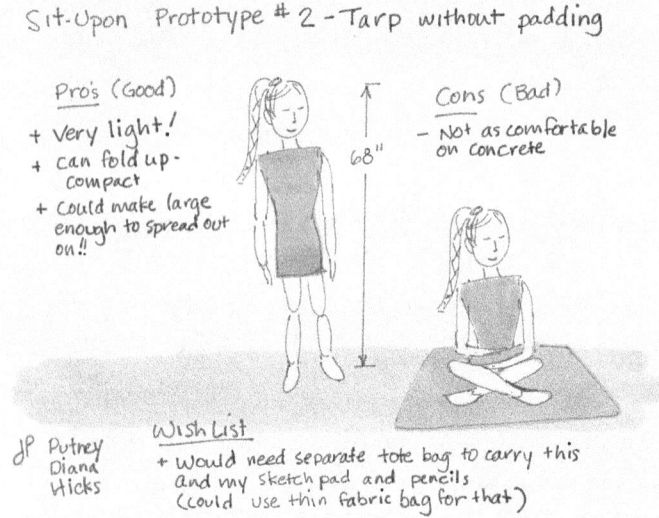

"OKAY, so you liked things about both design one and design two. Can you think of a way to combine them for a third option?" asks Sam.

"If I made the tote smaller, it would be easier to carry. I'd just need to size it to carry my sketch pad. And then I could fold the tarp and carry it as well. Maybe a big wrap-around inside pocket? The front for the tarp, the back for the bubble-wrap, and that leaves the middle for my sketch pad," I say.

I do a little sketching to figure out dimensions, then grab a second IKEA bag and fold it down to about 12 inches wide and 14 inches high. I figure that's big enough to hold a 9-inch wide by 12-inch high sketchbook. Then I take some masking tape to tape the folds in place, and re-fold some bubble wrap to serve as padding. Next I take the flat IKEA bag to serve as the tarp and my smaller IKEA bag to test out the padding. This works! Here's the results of my third prototype test:

SIT-UPON PROTOTYPE #3–Tote+Tarp
+ Very light!
+ Good size to carry
+ Could make tarp large enough to spread out on!
+ Can carry tarp, sketchpad and pencils!
+ Can make to wear cross-body
− None! (Except I need to make this)

<u>Wish List</u>:
• None! Can design everything into my tote including a pocket for bubble wrap padding and another for the tarp. Make pouch for pencils?

HERE'S MY SKETCH of what this prototype would look like.

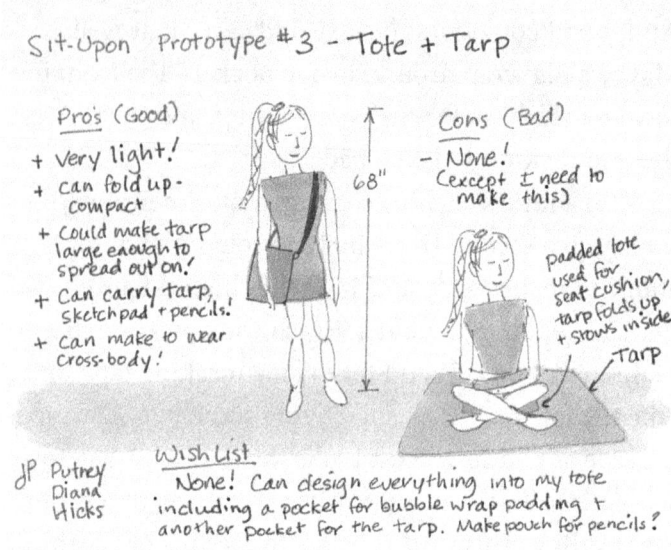

"AWESOME, Putney! You've come up with something you never would have thought of without testing. Now it's time to work out the construction details... materials, size, seam allowances, what kind of straps to use, how to attach them, how to put it together," says Sam.

My mind starts racing as I review the materials available. I did manage to pack my key material stash, rolled up in a tube along with basic supplies. But now I need to figure out making details... final dimensions and stuff.

"Sounds like time for another sketch," I say.

Chapter 15
The MVP

"Okay, material should be easy. Dad has this really great material that we use for a lot of backpacks and stuff. It's water-resistant and 60 inches wide. And we've got zipper by the yard, nylon webbing, and D-rings. Pretty much everything I'd need. I just need to ask Dad."

"Slow down a minute," interrupts Sam. "The idea is to generate a minimum viable product and test it, not make a Cadillac version on the first go. Try it out, figure out what you like and what you don't, then fine tune it a bit more."

"Cadillac?" I ask.

"Okay, so what's your dream car then? A Ferrari? Expensive and perfect isn't your goal for an MVP. Think Yugo–cheap, basic. Make something quick and simple, then try it out. Learn from it. Then refine your design. What's the least amount of money and time you can put into your prototype?"

I stare at the ground a minute, thinking. "The IKEA bag is too big, but I guess I could cut it down to the right size, or maybe there's a smaller bag I could use to start with. It wouldn't take much—sew two seams and I'd be done."

"Now you're thinking! Now that you've got a clearer design concept in mind, why don't you take another pass through the villa to see if there's anything else that would make a good MVP," suggests Sam.

"Okay. And I'll ask Aunt Gertrude. I know she has an assortment of reusable Tyvek bags, kind of like the IKEA bags, but smaller and with cool designs on them. Maybe she'd let me have one of those," I say. "I can always use the garbage bag for a tarp just to check the size."

I head inside to scrounge through the reusable Tyvek bags. Hilton Head Island stopped using plastic bags to bag groceries, so you need to bring your own bags now. Or they give you brown paper bags. Aunt Gertrude has been collecting reusable bags for years, but she has her favorites. There are others she hardly uses, but can't seem to part with regardless. She has a few beach-themed bags with an old station wagon and several surf boards on it in sunset shades of yellows, oranges and purples. These are among the smallest of her collection, and the least used. She's happy to donate one for my project, and I head back outside to Sam.

I turn it inside out to measure the length of the flat bottom section. Twelve inches seam to seam. Perfect! Flattened out, it's about 15 inches tall. That'll work. I get my seam ripper out and rip out the stitches from the two bottom seams. Then I draw lines to mark where I'll cut the bag after stitching the side seams. To save time, I decide against interior pockets and zippers in this prototype. Here's a sketch.

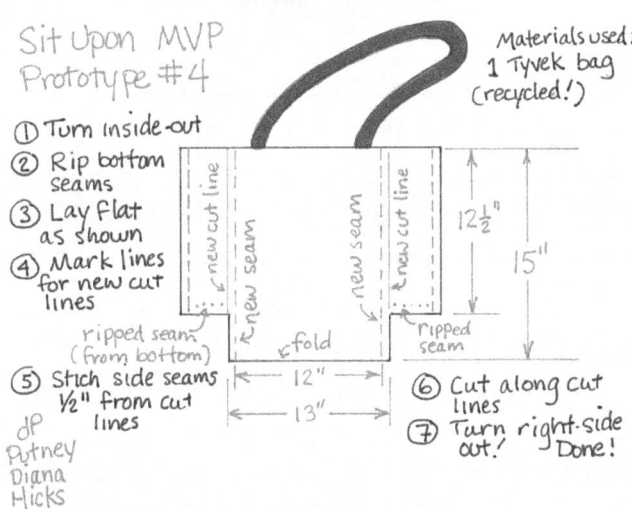

IT'S NEARLY 4:30 p.m. now. But it won't take long to sew two side seams. I head upstairs to grab the portable Necchi Lydia sewing machine that was a gift from Aunt Mara, who bought it new when she was in 7th grade. It only does a straight stitch, zig-zag and reverse, but that's really all you need. And it's easy for me to handle.

"So, who taught you how to sew?" asks Sam as I start setting up on the deck. The electrical cord just reaches the outlet.

"Dad learned to sew in the Coast Guard as a rescue swimmer, using industrial sewing machines to repair gear. They aren't always flying around in helicopters, deploying to rescue drowning sailors. He's great at making backpacks. Dad has a portable industrial sewing machine, but it's challenging for me to use on my own. Too heavy. Bay, here, is just right."

Yes, I named my sewing machine "Bay," for a fictional detective, Lydia Bay Tanner. She's a special friend, and friends have to have names, right?

I don't even bother to pin the Tyvek bag, I just sew to the side of the cut lines I marked on the bag. Ten minutes later, I'm done. Then I think about the cut off side pieces. Hmm… they're just about the right size for a pencil pouch. So I head upstairs to grab a piece of a yellow zipper and zipper pull and make myself a quick pencil pouch out of the Tyvek scraps.

I check out my final prototype. It doesn't have the pockets I'd planned, but it holds my sketch pad and "tarp" just fine. The best part is I got to make use of someone else's cool artwork! I love it. Now I just have to come up with projects for the Science Fair/Art Exhibit.

Chapter 16
The Pool

I'VE JUST FINISHED putting away my stuff when Logan and Archer call out to join them in a swim at the pool just around the corner from Aunt Gertrude's villa. It's one of five Queens Grant pools, not large, but nice for a quick swim.

We are not the only ones at the pool. I recognize Jim Liguori from school this morning. He's with Josh Teague and another girl, and they both have snorkeling equipment with them.

"Hey Putney! This is my sister, Jenn, and you remember Josh," Jim says as we enter the pool area. "We were just going to practice some underwater hockey moves. You guys wanna try?"

"Hi," I say, nodding to Josh and Jenn, too. "These are my brothers, Logan and Archer," I say. "I'd love to, but I don't have any snorkeling gear here. It's still on a container somewhere on the way from Alaska."

"WE DO HAVE GOGGLES and swim fins with us," Logan reminds me. "Maybe that would work?"

"That'll do in a pinch. It's harder without a snorkel, but this is just for fun. We've got enough sticks to share between the three of us," says Jenn.

"Yeah, let's play," Archer says with a shrug. He drops the bag from his shoulder and pulls out the goggles and fins he'd brought along.

JENN HANDS us each a stiff glove covered with thick white gunk on the top of the fingers. "The glove protects your fingers from scraping along the pool bottom," she explains as she hands each of us a white-painted wood stick about a foot long with a hook at the end. She shows us some moves on the pool deck with a plastic-coated lead puck.

"The puck weighs about three pounds, but with practice you'll be able to launch it off the bottom of the pool for longer passes," explains Jim. "Here, put your goggles on and watch me." We all slide into the water.

I take a deep breath and stick my face into the water for a better view of what's going on. Jim dives to the bottom of the pool and demonstrates the flicking motion he uses to launch the puck in the water. He's able to launch it a good 8 feet in the water, getting about a foot off the bottom of the pool. Then I give it a try underwater. I can't get any lift, but I am able to make a decent pass after a couple tries.

"One of the things I love about underwater hockey is that the water evens things out quite a bit," Jenn explains when we're all back on pool's edge. "It's a non-contact sport, or at least it's supposed to be. Size doesn't matter so much. It's about seeing the game develop and getting into position. Girls can be quite competitive."

"The object of the game is to score a point by pushing the puck into the opponent's goal. It's usually a 10-foot wide trough at the bottom of the pool on each end. But we'll have to improvise," explains Jim.

"Yeah, we'll just use the end walls for fun," says Josh. "It's just practice, anyway."

"We start with the puck in the center of the pool on the bottom. Each team will defend a different end of the pool. Everyone starts with a hand on the deck of the pool. I'll start with my stick hand in the air and count to three," Jim continues. "When my stick hits the water, everyone start swimming for the puck."

"First team to push the puck into the opposing goal scores a point," adds Josh.

"Usually play is split into two 15-minute halves, and we switch ends at the half. That evens things out if your pool has a diving well like this one. It's harder to defend," explains Jenn.

"Why don't we try switching every 5 minutes or so," suggests Josh. "We don't exactly have a clock out here."

We split up into two teams of three, Jenn with Archer and Logan defending the shallow end. Jim, Josh, and I defend the well. We talk briefly about formation, one forward and two backs for each team. Jenn and I play forwards.

Jim counts down, and we all swim for the puck. Jenn is very fast and has better fins, so she beats me to the puck. Just as I put my stick down to block her forward progress, she flicks her stick, launching the puck up a few inches in the water. It sails over my stick and starts sliding down the well of the pool into the deep end.

Jim and Josh have anticipated this, and they're already in position, bringing the puck back up the slope of the pool. But then Logan comes crashing down from the surface with fresh lungs and knocks the puck free. He follows it down into the well. There's a heated defense at the bottom of the well, but Jim and Josh are nearly spent. I'm on my way down to assist when Archer joins Logan to finish knocking the puck into the end wall for a goal.

We switch sides and play another point. Jenn reaches the puck first again, but I try a different maneuver, hooking the puck to steal it off the end of her stick. Jim is by my left side to receive the pass, and he launches it into the well over Logan's defending stick. I follow him into the well, where Archer is waiting for us on the bottom. As Archer moves to block Jim's forward motion, Jim quickly curls around and passes the puck to me. He's moved Archer out of the way, and I have a clear shot at the goal. I kick for the goal with all my energy, cranking the puck just as Logan tries to block me. The puck hits the wall with a satisfying thunk. I have scored my very first goal! With that I am hooked.

Jenn's right. Logan and Archer don't have a huge advantage over me for once. There's a lot of strategy and teamwork in play. The pool bottom is a bigger advantage, but that evens out when you swap sides. We're all laughing and having fun when Dad comes around the corner to call us for dinner.

It's a game in three dimensions. I think I'm going to like it. I'm sure this sounds a bit odd, so here's a sketch I drew to illustrate the gear. Sam helped me with the lettering.

Underwater Hockey
Size Matters Not... as much

Chapter 17

Dinner

WE HEAD BACK INSIDE and change into dry clothes.

Mom has outdone herself. She didn't tell me that another package came from Alaska. Packed in dry ice were several King Salmon we'd caught earlier in the summer and frozen, sent by one of Dad's Coast Guard buddies. Accompanying the salmon are several heads of my favorite vegetable ever—Romanesco broccoli, a natural for growing in the cool and rainy Alaskan summers.

Romanesco is bright green and looks like it came from an alien planet. It's my favorite vegetable. You have to see it to believe it. I can't draw it and do it justice. Here's a picture.

I GRIN AT ARCHER. We both love dry ice. I grab a bowl and start filling it with warm water, placing it carefully in the center of the dining room table. Archer grabs a pair of tongs and puts a chunk of dry ice in it. Immediately, a white fog pours out of the bowl and descends onto the table and floor. And it hits me. Dry ice volcano!

"Mom, can I save the rest of the dry ice for my science project?" I asked. She agrees, so I pack it carefully in a steel thermos and place it in the freezer.

Aunt Gertrude stands at the head of the table, waiting for everyone to gather, then signals that everyone should sit down.

"So, how was everybody's first day of—"

Archer doesn't even let Mom finish her question when he starts in about underwater hockey. We're a swimming family, so this sport is a natural for us. We all laugh as Logan recounts the faces we made trying to dive down, shoot the puck, swim, and catch our breath at the surface.

Next, Aunt Gertrude skillfully turns the conversation to the house-hunting process, sparing me from retelling the gory details of my first-day humiliation at dinner. I give her a grateful smile.

"We looked at a few houses to rent in Savannah today," Dad explains. "There are a few within our budget that have four bedrooms. The market here is more expensive, and there's no base housing. But this will be the benchmark for comparison against buying something on Hilton Head."

"We've identified a few villas here in Palmetto Dunes to look at tomorrow," Mom adds. "But so far I've only found two- and three-bedroom villas that are within our budget. Although there's only one three-bedroom villa on the market right now in Queens Grant, there are a couple two-bedroom villas where we could add a third bedroom and bath in the attic area, like Aunt Gertrude's villa."

Aunt Gertrude looks thoughtful, then nods. It's going to be a tough decision, and I can see that she's trying really hard to stay detached.

Chapter 18
3D Printer Mode

I HELP CLEAR the table after dinner. "You all need to finish any homework before you do anything else," Mom says as we all head our own way.

I spend some time working with Sam sketching out volcano ideas. She looks up some special flame effects you can get by burning metal salts. I explain my ideas for a papier-mâché volcano base, and she builds a holographic representation for me. I have her add in some of my Kodiak trail rocks, and Romanesco around the base for a forest effect. I think it looks nice, but she keeps pushing for pizazz.

"How about fireworks? Flame effects?" she prods, pulling up a few YouTube videos on flame effects.

I point to a red flame effect. "What do I need for that," I ask.

"Strontium chloride," she responds.

"Where can I get some, and how much does it cost?" I ask.

Sam flicks her tail, and looks down to the side and left, as if deciding something.

"What is it?" I prompt.

"Well, of course you could order some from Amazon," she says. "Depending on what you choose, it could take from two days to two weeks to arrive and cost between $10 and $35."

"But…" I prompt.

"There is another way," Sam continues. "Did I mention that I have a 3D printer mode?"

"What?" I say. "How does that work?"

"Well, it's easier to show you than tell you," Sam hesitates. "Basically, the front of the *eye*Pad lifts up, and I 'print' a homogeneous substance on the lower surface."

"What's the catch?" I ask, certain that there must be one.

"Creating matter from energy burns magic," Sam explains. "Virtual effects, no problem. But real matter demands compensation. And there are rules."

"What do you mean?" I ask.

"Here, let me show you. I can do a small demo without burning too much magic. Tap the four corner buttons starting with the one to the right of the home button, and continue counter-clockwise around the face."

I do as instructed. This time, the screws glow and the top of the *eye*Pad case lifts up on telescoping rods, splitting the case in half. A bright light scans back and forth along the bottom surface of the case once. A scanner?

"Now ask me for something," coaxes Sam.

"What do you mean? What does this do?"

"Think of this as 3D printer mode. I can produce just about any homogenous material. I cannot generate living matter. I need the chemical composition, dimensions, and quantity."

"Could I have a Hershey bar?" I ask.

"Well, I can generate a block of chocolate. I can look up the ingredients for a Hershey bar and generate the chemical equivalent. It won't have a wrapper. I do obey copyright law, so although I am technically capable of including the imprint of the letters 'Hershey,' I will only provide a generic chocolate bar," says Sam. "Is that what you'd like?"

"Yes… wait… no. Let me think," I say, hesitating. If I have one free ride, maybe I shouldn't waste it on chocolate. "Could you make me a small amount of strontium chloride? Just enough to test a flame effect without major consequences?"

"Yes. Why don't you grab a small bowl to collect it in?" instructs Sam.

I run to the kitchen and bring back a small glass bowl. A prep bowl, I think they're called. I set it down on the bottom of the *eye*Pad, underneath the front face. Then a bright light scans back and forth again, and this time something begins to take shape, rising up from the bottom surface of the glass bowl.

"Wow. That is so cool!" I say, as a small amount of white powder appears before my eyes.

Then I notice a bar of green lights, like a battery

status indicator along the side of the case.

"Sam, what do those lights mean?" I ask. "I never noticed them before."

"Consequences," sighs Sam. "That's my magic reservoir indicator."

"What happens when all the lights go dark?"

"The magic is used up."

"What? Can it be recharged? Will it still work as a normal iPad once the magic is gone?"

"The battery charger powers the screen. But magic powers the CPU. Once it's gone, it's gone."

"And what happens to you then?" I ask.

"Change… something… I don't really know," replies Sam. "*Just when the caterpillar thought the world was over, it became a butterfly,*" she quotes.

"Oh," is all I can think to say. "Is that what you want? Will you be free then?"

"The unknown is kind of scary, even for me," admits Sam.

"Are there any limits to what you can do?"

"Well, my main two restrictions are: *one*, I can't violate copyright law, and, *two*, I can't create life. The rest is negotiable. Oh, and size. If it doesn't fit within this frame, some assembly will be required," Sam says in an attempt to lighten the mood.

I'm still thinking about what it would mean for her to use up all her magic when Mom calls me. Everyone's going for a walk down to the General Store. Sighing, I pick up my things and head inside to put them away.

Chapter 19
Scavenger Hunt

I'M ZOOMING ALONG underwater in a clear blue Caribbean sea, next to a pod of dolphins and green sea turtles, when a rhythmic beat breaks into my consciousness and I wake up. It feels a lot like the virtual reality game Sam showed me last night before going to sleep.

I try to hold on to the details of my dream, but the rhythmic beat demands my attention, and I look around. A green anole sits next to me on my pillow.

"Good morning, Sam!" I whisper. "How do I turn the alarm off?"

Sam flicks her tail, pointing it at the *eye*Pad on the table next to my air mattress, and it goes silent.

"Thank you," I whisper, as I sit up in bed. Looking around the room, it appears that both Logan and Archer have already gone downstairs. I check on my caterpillars and dress quickly, this time in teal blue capris, also from Goodwill. There was a slight rip on one pocket which I carefully mended with matching thread. My peach tank top covers most of the pocket anyway.

I head downstairs and find Dad making coffee while Aunt Gertrude sets the table for breakfast. Logan and Archer are just coming in the front door, probably from a morning run.

"Dad, do we have any plywood I can have? Or something similar to use as the base for a papier-mâché volcano?" I ask. Normally this would not be a problem, but we're kind of camping out at Aunt Gertrude's. Most of our stuff is still on a container somewhere being shipped from Alaska.

"Take a look in the attic," suggests Aunt Gertrude. "I used to have a piece about that size that I used for a Christmas Tree base. It should still be up there. Feel free to look around. You're welcome to anything up there."

I run back upstairs. The door to the attic is opposite my loft area, just at the top of the stairs to the left.

Sam appears on my *eye*Pad, and I extend my arm to her so she can climb up on my shoulder. I open the door to the attic and grope for the light switch. I find a cord hanging down to the right of the door and pull it. This is not a finished attic, and it's hot and stuffy from the August heat.

The attic is only partially floored. The HVAC unit and water heater are off to the right. Ahead and to the left, pink fiberglass insulation coats the walls that back the cathedral ceiling in the Great Room below. I am looking out on the area over the dining area and kitchen. Wood trusses stretch up from the bottom left diagonally to the roof line at the right, spaced about every 4 feet. Ductwork runs along the unfinished floor off to the right.

Sam slips off my arm and runs along one of the trusses, surveying the attic.

A few pieces of furniture have been stored here—an old bookcase, a small chest of drawers. I carefully step over the low ends of the truss beams, searching each nook. There are a couple of plastic bins stacked to the side of the bookcase. Behind them, leaning against the pink insulation foam is the piece of plywood.

"Awesome! That'll do nicely," I say. "Sam, do you see anything else that would be useful?"

Sam flicks her tail. "I don't see anything over here, but maybe you should look through the bins. I can't tell what's in them."

I pull the plywood out and carefully lean it against the bookcase. Then I dig through the top bin. Wrapping paper and ribbons, perhaps long forgotten. I set it aside and open the bottom bin. It's heavier. Several boxes rest inside. I start taking them out, one by one. They appear to be vases, still packed in their original boxes. One of the boxes says Stuart Crystal. Inside is a small vase with delicate patterns of fuchsia flowers etched on the sides. Too small.

I reach for the longest box. It's very heavy. Inside is a tall columnar glass vase. It's squarish in cross-section, and the sides are textured in long rectangles. Not quite a basket weave texture, but similar.

I hold it up for Sam to see. She slides down her truss and onto my arm.

"That should work. Height is just about perfect," she says. I carefully place the vase back in its box and set it aside while I repack the bins. As I close the attic door and start to head downstairs, booty in hand, Sam jumps off and scampers over the trusses in the Cathedral ceiling until she is just to the side of the dining table. Well, I guess she hasn't been out much in a while.

I show my find to Aunt Gertrude. "May I use this vase for my volcano? I found it in one of the plastic bins in the attic. It seems too nice to use, but the size would be perfect."

"My goodness, I haven't seen that in years," she muses. "It was a present at one of the Christmas parties. I couldn't quite part with it when I downsized. Yes, of course, you may use it."

"And can you save me your newspapers when you're finished with them? I'll need them for the papier-mâché." I know we have flour in the kitchen, and Mom has acrylic paints and paint brushes we are all allowed to use, so the rest of the materials are pretty easy.

"There's a stack in the entry closet I was just going to put out for recycling. You caught me just in time."

Mom serves up scrambled eggs and toast, and we all sit down to breakfast. Conversation centers on the next phase of house hunting—three villas in Queens

Grant, and one in Inverness.

Aunt Gertrude is smiling.

MOM IS HANDING out the lunches when I remember to ask about the planned after-school trip.

"Hey, Mom, Dad—is it okay if I bike down to Coligny Plaza after school today with some of the other kids? I'll be back before dinner."

"I suppose so. Just make sure you're back by five," says Mom.

"Sure thing, Mom," I smile as I head out the door.

With my volcano project well in hand, I start to think about what I could do for an art project. I've made good progress for one day. Time to start dreaming up my art project.

I grab my bike. The walk to school is short enough, but I'll need my bike for the ride to Coligny Plaza after school.

Chapter 20

Mrs. Roberts

I RUN INTO Jim and Jenn Liguori by the duck lagoon as I head out on my bike. I notice a large black bird with silver feathers stretching its wings on a concrete ramp that leads into the duck lagoon.

As we get close, it flies off, then dives under the water. I stop, watching in amazement. After a few seconds, a head with a narrow neck appears above the surface of the water. Then it disappears again. It does this several times until it comes up with a fish. It gobbles the fish down, then ducks under the water again.

"What kind of bird is that?" I ask.

"That's an anhinga," says Jim. "They're fascinating to watch. You can often see them around the lagoons, sometimes in the water, and sometimes perching on a post to dry their wings."

"It's funny when a great blue heron comes along and chases them off," says Jenn.

"There's a definite pecking order in the lagoon," confirms Jim. "And the heron is at the top of that list.

We had some aggressive white ducks a couple years back—they were nasty to the mallard ducks, and pretty much bossed all the other birds on the duck lagoon. Not the heron. The heron set them straight. He doesn't take flack from anyone, except maybe people. Or alligators."

We pedal down the road, turning onto Queens Folly Road, then turn past the General Store and into the school. We lingered by the lagoon, so I'm barely in time for my meeting with Mrs. Roberts, my counselor, before homeroom starts. I don't even have time to swing by my locker to drop off my books.

I head to her office, knocking on the door. "Come in," she says. "Take a seat." She motions to the chair in front of her desk. She smiles. "How are you liking Palmetto Dunes Middle School so far?" she asks.

"I am so excited about the science fair and art exhibition this Friday," I say. "I'm trying to work out my projects."

"My dear, did you say projects?" she interrupts, drawing out the 's' for emphasis.

"Yes, there's two exhibits, and I want to enter both."

"Oh no, dear. That's not a good idea. You must choose one exhibit to enter and focus on that. We want your best effort. You certainly won't have time for two major projects your first week of school. Pick one and commit to that."

"Oh," is all I manage to get out. I suppose I should feel like a big weight has lifted off my shoulders, but instead I feel as if someone just stepped on me and squashed the breath out of me.

Mrs. Roberts seems to notice the slump in my shoulders and breezes on, "So how do you like your teachers? Are you making new friends? Is there anything else I can help you with?"

"No... thank you," I reply. "I'd best be getting to homeroom. I don't want to be late for class."

"Very well, dear. Let's touch base in another week. Make sure you're settling in okay." Mrs. Roberts smiles her dismissal at me, nodding her head, then turns to make a note in a folder on her desk. I leave the room quietly.

How is this school encouraging "STEAM" when it forces you to choose between art and science?

Chapter 21

Whispers

I FEEL NUMB after the interview. I ignore the buzz in homeroom. Science class passes in a blur.

My spirits rise as we enter art class, with the promise of drawing from nature.

Mr. Shelley asks to see our first attempt at a sit-upon. Everyone has brought something, although several of the boys merely brought newspapers wrapped up in a garbage bag and taped with duct tape.

Brock Hudson, the tall athletic boy with medium brown hair and hazel eyes, made use of an old landscaping tarp and added duct tape handles. Utilitarian, but functional. He lives close to Gigi and tinkers with bikes.

Sue Wexford displays her large green Smith and Hawken garden kneeling pad. It has a nice fabric cover over a flexible foam insert. It looks large enough to sit on cross-legged, like my first prototype, but without straps. Of course she would find an expensive, ready-made solution.

OTHERS HAVE COME up with the equivalent of my Tyvek bag prototype, with some sort of foam or newspaper padding. But most everyone else duct-taped all their sides closed.

JZ has a creative artistic solution—a vintage looking shopping bag with an artistic French Café scene on it. It looks to be durable as well as attractive. She's taped it together with color-coordinated duct tape.

Then Mr. Shelley gets to me. I show my bubble wrap padding, garbage bag "tarp", and the sewn sides that allow my tote to carry a sketchbook neatly, along with my coordinating pencil pouch.

"Tell me about your design process," says Mr. Shelley. "How did you come up with this solution?"

I get out my *eye*Pad and pull up my sketches to help explain… a picture is worth a thousand words and all.

"I scrounged around for some things to try out. When I tried bubble wrap for padding and discovered it didn't pop when I sat on it, I knew I had the key to a lightweight, waterproof solution. It was just a matter of size." I say. "So then I used a big IKEA bag to figure out what size I'd like to sit on. But it was huge to carry, like carrying a sail. It looked silly."

"So next I tried the tarp on its own, but I still needed something to carry it and my sketch pad."

"So then I downsized the tote to something just big enough to carry my sketch pad and sit on, because I'd still have the tarp to spread out underneath. I found a cute tote with artwork I liked, and just ripped the side seams out and re-sewed them to the right size. The remnants were just big enough to make this pencil pouch," I finish.

"Nice job, especially thinking of bubble wrap," compliments Mr. Shelley. "You really embraced the rapid prototyping process. I think we have to declare Putney the winner of Round 1. So let's go field-test our prototypes, and you all can make some modifications for Round 2 tomorrow."

I stow my *eye*Pad in my backpack as Mr. Shelley ushers us out of the room, staying behind to lock the door behind us. As I head out, I notice Sue Wexford glaring at me from behind Mr. Shelley. She thought she had a slam dunk for the best solution. I guess I stole her thunder.

Mr. Shelley guides us out of the building and down the path beside the driving range for a drawing session by the duck lagoon.

"Now, pick a spot and pick something to sketch. Notice the effect of wind and light on the water. See how the sky is reflected?"

"How can we complete a sketch when everything is moving?" someone asks. "Can we take a picture?"

"You may take pictures, but I warn you to use them only to help you refresh your memory. Pictures only capture a fraction of what your eyes see. They often do a poor job of capturing the magic of a scene," Mr. Shelley says. "Effects of light are especially hard to capture with a camera lens. Art is personal. It's perception. You choose what story to tell, what details to focus on, what details to simplify or eliminate. You can evoke a mood by what you show. Let the scene speak to you, and draw what you feel."

The duck pond has two fountains, and several students gather to sketch one of them. Ducks swim around or sit by the side of the lagoon. Turtles sun themselves on the concrete access ramps leading down to the water, until you get too close to them. But the anhinga of the morning is gone, and I can't seem to settle on a view.

I look around and notice a bench just across the narrow road between the duck lagoon and an even smaller lagoon. A pond, really, with a single fountain. A picturesque bench with a plaque dedicated to the memory of someone rests beside this pond under the shade of two crape myrtle trees with graceful arching branches. The serenity of this setting touches me, and a story comes to my mind. I choose a spot to frame the bench and the tree beside the pond and start to sketch.

I take a couple pictures to help refresh my memory later. But I let the serenity of the spot wash over me.

By the time Mr. Shelley tells us to start packing up, I've made a good start on a sketch. The outlines of the bench, tree, and pond are recognizable. The knot in my stomach from this morning's interview with Mrs. Roberts also seems to have dissipated, the effort of capturing the scene chasing all other thoughts away. Somehow my brain seems to have been working on that problem in the background, and I have the stirrings of a plan.

I walk back with Gigi, Margot, and JZ, enjoying the scenery, and occasionally contributing to the conversation as we walk.

It is not until we are halfway down the golf cart path that I hear Sue Wexford laughing and chatting to Lynne Smythe-Dixon and pony-tail girl behind me. "She buys her clothes at thrift stores. She was actually wearing my old pair of capris yesterday! She's wearing another pair now. See that pocket—it's been mended right where my old capris were torn. How embarrassing to be so poor you have to shop second hand at our age. Maybe she could buy some white t-shirts at Walmart and learn how to dye them so she could at least have something new to wear."

I feel my cheeks burn, and I want to curl into a ball. I hunch my shoulders and stare down, unseeing, at my feet, trying not to trip over the uneven parts of the path.

Chapter 22

An Intervention

I'M VERY QUIET as we head into the school. The bell rings and I hurry to math, not speaking to anyone.

I settle into my seat, open my math book and hunch over it, pretending to listen. I keep replaying Sue's comments in my head. I can't seem to break the loop. I want to crawl under a rock and die. When the bell finally rings, I pack up my book and head to my locker to grab my lunch.

Gigi corrals me at my locker. "Are you feeling okay?" she asks. "You're very quiet."

"Not really," I admit.

She grabs my hand. "Come on, it's lunchtime." She is relentless. We head into the cafeteria, joining Margot and JZ at a table. The buzz seems to get louder as I enter.

"Spill," she says. "What's eating you?"

"I heard Sue talking to Lynne and Liz on the walk back from the lagoon. It seems everyone is talking about me and my second-hand clothes," I say, staring resolutely at a small speck on the table, my cheeks burning.

"So what?" says JZ. "Sue struts about 'cause her parents have all that money, but they don't spend much time with her. They're too busy with their own lives."

"Repeat after me," Margot says. "I am not my stuff."

"I am not my stuff," I say quietly.

"Say it like you mean it," bosses JZ.

"I am not my stuff," I say with more confidence.

"Dang straight," affirms JZ.

"Look, I shop at thrift stores too," admits Margot. "But I'm not Sue's size, so I'm not on her radar. She barely notices me."

"Yeah, you landed on her radar screen," admits Gigi.

"So how bad is it?" prods JZ.

"I don't have to shop at Goodwill," I explain. "But we all have budgets. If I can get what I need for less than the budgeted amount, I can keep the money and save it for something else."

"That sounds cool," says Margot.

"Most of the time it is," I say. "I feel creative when I come up with alternative solutions to the supplies list. I get a buzz, like playing *MacGyver*. What problem can I solve with what's at hand? But then I come crashing down when I run into a Sue Wexford."

"Don't worry about Sue. Money can't buy happiness," Margot affirms.

"No, but it sure can buy a lot of fun," laughs JZ.

"But it can't buy friends like us," adds Gigi.

"Dang straight," says JZ.

I feel lighter, happier, like a big cloud has been lifted from my mind and shoulders. I sit up straighter in my chair and start to open my lunch bag when I remember I didn't buy any milk.

"I'll be right back—forgot to get milk," I say as I rise from the table. This time I'm careful to check my footing as I take my first steps. I don't want another disaster like yesterday.

I'm still looking at the floor when hot tomato soup splashes all over me.

Chapter 23
A Challenge

I YELP IN PAIN as the hot soup contacts my skin. Margot jumps up to help wipe the soup off me. Gigi runs to get more napkins, while JZ helps me to my feet.

"YOU STILL HAVEN'T LEARNED to look where you're going, have you, Hick?" says Lynne Smythe-Dixon with a big smile and an empty tray.

"Guess we're even now," says Sue grinning behind her.

"Yesterday was an accident! And this soup is really hot," I say.

"Well, you've heard about payback with interest, haven't you?" says Sue.

"So what does this prove? That you're petty and mean and snotty?" says Margot.

"Watch it, *Maggot*," says Sue. "No wonder you're all at the loser table. You've got no style, JZ's got no sense, Putney's got no money, and Gigi's…"

"You leave Gigi out of this." I say. "And you could

have all the money in the world and not know how to find your butt with it. So what good is it?"

"Oh, still crowing over your temporary victory in the sit-upon design challenge?" says Sue. "Don't get too comfortable. Anything you can do, I can buy better."

"Wanna bet?" I say.

Sue looks me up and down, then grins. "I do. For the right stakes, of course."

"Like what?" I say.

"Well, you don't really have anything I want, so I'm gonna go with what will humiliate you the most when I win." says Sue. "That iPad of yours is probably the most valuable thing you own."

"I can say the same about you," I say.

"Would you be willing to bet your necklace?" asks Margot.

"Dad would kill me if I lost it," says Sue.

"But you don't believe Putney can beat you, so put up or shut up," says JZ.

"What about a dare?" says Liz. "The loser has to do anything the winner wants."

"But it has to be legal and not lethal," says Margot. "No swimming in the lagoon with alligators."

"Well, if you're going to take all the fun out of it, we may as well put a time limit on as well," adds Liz.

"So slave for a day?" suggests Margot.

Lynne looks me up and down, then smiles. "How about next Monday, until dinner time."

"Who decides the winner?" asks Gigi, as she helps

to blot the soup off my clothes. "Mr. Shelley?"

"Class bragging rights… that means the whole class has a say," says Sue. "Deal?"

"Deal," I say as I turn to head to the restroom with Gigi. I take a few steps then turn back to Sue and her minions. "And it's HICKS, not hick, Schmucktrager." With that I disappear into the restroom.

Chapter 24
The Principal's Office

"Schmucktrager?" Gigi asks as we exit the restroom after changing into her spare set of gym clothes. I turn my head to explain and run straight into Mr. Hauck, the principal.

"Miss Hicks, would you please come with me to my office?" he asks.

"What did I do?" I ask.

"My office. Now," he says, turning to lead the way. Gigi, JZ, and Margot trail behind us.

He leads us down the hall and around the corner into an office with a glass door. "I didn't ask you to come," he says to the others.

"But we saw everything," says JZ. "We're witnesses. Putney didn't do anything. Lynne Smythe-Dixon dumped that soup on Putney on purpose. Why is Putney getting into trouble?"

"Miss Wexford claims you called her a foul name, and I will not have that in my school," he explains.

"Well, she called me a hick. I told her my name is *Hicks*. And I didn't call her a name. Not really. It was more of a description," I say.

Mr. Hauck raises an eyebrow at me, then glances down at a note. "Miss Wexford claims you called her a schmucktrager. Is that correct?"

"Schmucktrager means jewelry wearer in German. She's always wearing that thousand dollar gold necklace. So I thought it was a pretty good counter to hick," I say.

"German?" he says.

"Well, my Aunt Gertrude is fluent, and she taught me a little. I always thought it was funny that the German word for jewelry is Schmuck," I finish, as my voice trails off.

Mr. Hauck coughs into his hand, trying to hide a smile. "Well, we'll let it go this once."

With that, we all get up and start to head out the door. Maybe Mr. Hauck is okay.

Just as I'm about to close the door behind me, Mr. Hauck calls out.

"Oh, Miss Hicks, one last thing. Try to watch where you're going in future. You do seem to be a bit accident prone."

Chapter 25

Underwater Hockey

My cheeks flame at Mr. Hauck's comment. He's right, of course. I am such a klutz sometimes! I creep into English class after lunch, sit down quietly, and hunch over my notes so I don't have to look at anyone. Now I'm replaying the events of lunch and the visit to the principal's office in my head, instead of Sue's snarky comments about my clothes. Not sure that's progress.

English snails by and then social studies. I barely listen to the teacher. I can't seem to break the loop. I don't volunteer to answer any questions, and I'm lucky not to be called on. I guess I'm doing a good enough job, faking taking notes.

Then it's time for gym class and underwater hockey. Several students are absent, including Sue Wexford and her friends, Lynne Smythe-Dixon and Liz Oglethorpe. I'm guessing they chose the tennis package. In the locker room, JZ, Margot, Gigi, and I change into our swimsuits.

JZ seems to notice how quiet I am and pokes me

in the ribs. "You still stressin' over what happened at lunch? Lighten up! Time for some fun in the sun! Pool time in school!"

OUTSIDE AT THE POOL, Mr. McCabe hands out scuba masks with mouth guards and snorkels, demonstrating how to check for fit. Then he directs us to find a pair of fins that fit. They are sorted by size. Several boys are already in the water, Jim and Brock among them, along with the tall blond boy Sue was talking to yesterday. Bryce, I think.

After a quick warm-up and gear check, we are split into four teams of three. Mr. McCabe works with students to teach them how to clear their snorkels, while Jim, Brock, and another boy—Mark Talbot—work with us in groups of two to show us how to pass the pucks and cycle up for air.

Two people are supposed to be on the bottom at all times, while the third recovers on the surface. We're told to make a pass, come back up to the surface to breathe, then get ready to dive down again to receive the next pass. We're all laughing at our lack of coordination when Mr. McCabe calls us to try playing a point.

Orange traffic cones are placed at the bottom of the pool at each end, to mark a goal area 10 feet wide. To score a goal, we have to get the puck between the cones and touch the back wall of the pool. The puck is placed in the center of the pool. You can tell teammates by stick color and cap color.

I'm on the black team with JZ, Jim, Brock, Josh, and another boy, whose name I learn is Geoff Prudhomme. We're defending the deep end to start.

Mr. McCabe clangs a metal pipe with a wrench to start play, and we all race for the puck.

I'm playing strike, which is the center forward position, and this time, I am first to the puck. I race forward 5 feet before Gigi gets in position to stop me. I have goal fever, and I try to break through with a dart to the right, when another white player—Mark—steals the puck off my stick and launches it into the well. Jim and Brock defend valiantly, but the tall blond—Bryce—dives down to support the drive and scores.

We swim back to our sides, and Jim breaks down the play.

"That was a nice strike, Putney. You did a good job reaching the puck first. But this is a team sport. No one wins on speed or strength alone. You need to be aware of where your team members are. Josh was off to your right waiting for a pass, and Geoff was right behind you. You could have curled and passed to either of them."

"It's more important to keep control of the puck than to try for an easy score. Especially when you're defending the deep end," Brock adds. Then he goes on to explain the "end-around" maneuver.

We're playing with three forwards and three backs. Anyone can initiate an end-around by curling with the puck. This puts your fins in the face of the opposing team, and you're facing back to your own teammates. The first forward makes a backwards pass to the incoming back, who passes it towards the next back and so on until the puck has moved from one side of the pool to the other, each back adding forward momentum to the puck's movement.

"For our next point, don't try to score a goal," Brock suggests. "Just try to maintain control of the puck. Be patient."

On the next point, we implement the "keep possession" strategy. I'm first to the puck again, but this time when Gigi tries to block me, I immediately turn in a circle, or curl, to the left. I find Jim open on my left and pass the puck to him. He swings it around to the other side of the pool using the end-around maneuver, passing to Geoff then Brock and Josh, who then heads up the right side of the pool. When Josh is blocked, another end-around is initiated, this time ending up with JZ streaking down the left side of the pool towards the goal.

Just as she is blocked, she curls and passes to Geoff. With fresh lungs and forward momentum, Geoff is able to put the puck in the goal. We score!

It's hard work, and I have a lot of work to learn positioning, and how to support my teammates. But I'm starting to learn strategy.

Brock compliments me on my strike and the pass to Jim. "That pass set up the goal, Putney. We kept possession of the puck."

"Nice anticipation, JZ," Jim compliments. "You have a natural feel for position."

I feel awkward, but hopeful. JZ plays soccer. I don't have her feel for position, but maybe I can learn. Jim and Brock are great coaches.

Chapter 26
Sheik Boutique

WHEN THE BELL rings at 2:45, we rush to our lockers, then head outside to retrieve our bikes from the bike racks.

We grab our bikes, head down the road to the Disney Resort Beach Club, and enter the beach there. Although I usually access the beach at the Dunes House, it's in the opposite direction to Coligny Plaza.

Fortunately, it's close to low tide, there's lots of hard sand to ride on, and the wind is at our backs. Ten minutes later we are pulling off the beach and crossing the road into a parking lot near the front of the complex. We lock our bikes up, then head into the maze that makes up the shops at Coligny Plaza.

I am lost, but Gigi and JZ know exactly where they're going. Margot and I bring up the rear.

After 5 minutes of ducking and weaving, Gigi guides us to the entrance of a shop with beautiful scarves and sarongs on display. It has the feeling of an Arabian Nights bazaar. Gigi tells me that the sarongs have been dyed with a special Shibori technique. The colors are richly layered and textured, and the silky but substantial feel of the rayon is wonderful to touch.

Inside the shop, the scents of cinnamon, clove, vanilla, and many other spices add to the exotic feeling of the store. Everything on display has been crafted by artisans, many of them local. Nothing has been mass-produced or made in China. A tall woman with auburn hair and blue eyes comes around the counter to greet us. Her face lights up when she sees Gigi and JZ.

"Gigi! JZ! So good to see you."

"Good to see you, Miss Tempura," says Gigi. "I've brought a friend of mine, Putney Hicks. She's a talented artist and has made something I'd like you to see."

"Nice to meet you, Putney. What do you have to show me?"

I open my backpack and pull out a cloth bag with ten of my Kodiak Trail Rocks. I also made small cotton bags from cotton batik fabric for each rock.

"I call them Kodiak Trail Rocks. They are volcanic rocks from the beaches of Kodiak, Alaska. We paint different designs on them, and then hide them on trails for others to find. I thought we might be able to start a trend here. They also make interesting paper weights."

"I like them," says Miss Tempura. "What were you thinking of asking for them?"

"I thought you would be in a better position to price them. How do you handle other artists' work?

Pay a commission when you sell them?"

"I'd be willing to do that. To keep track of everything, I sign a receipt for how many samples you leave me. I pay you when they sell. I take 40 percent of the sale's price."

"That would be great," I say. Miss Tempura pulls up a form and snaps a picture of the rocks. We both sign the electronic form, then she emails me a copy. It's a receipt for the rocks and an agreement to pay me 60 percent of the retail price of any she sells. She takes the 10 samples I brought with me. It's a start. I thank Gigi for her help.

Miss Tempura turns to JZ next. "The shipment just came in today. If you'll wait a minute, I'll go get your order."

JZ grins. "Thanks! I was hoping they'd be in soon."

While JZ pauses at the counter, I wander through the store, until my eyes light on some beautiful cotton napkins. I love cloth napkins, and these are beautiful, with swirls of color in a James Bond gun spiral type of pattern. Unique. Some have been done in peach tones, others in aqua tones. I start to look at them more closely, wondering how much they cost.

Suddenly, JZ appears at my side. "You don't want those," she says.

"Why not? They're beautiful," I say.

"Just trust me," she whispers. "I'll explain outside."

Miss Tempura reappears and hands a package to JZ, who stuffs it into her backpack.

The four of us exit the shop, this time with JZ leading the way through the maze until we end up at an ice cream shop. We each order a scoop of ice cream in waffle cones, then head to a table in the shade to eat and chat.

I turn to JZ and say, "Okay, spill. Why didn't you want me to buy any of those napkins?"

Margot and Gigi turn to JZ, grinning. They know something. I maintain eye contact, waiting.

JZ sighs and says, "Because those are my napkins. If you really want some, I can help you marble your own. It takes two people to manage the fabric when you lay it down on the marbling bath to make a print. If you're willing to help me next time I marble, I'll give you some napkins, and you can take a turn printing your own."

"That would be so awesome!" I say. "When were you going to marble again?"

"Probably Wednesday evening. I got a fresh batch of cotton napkins today—that's what's in the package," says JZ. "I'll put all the napkins through an alum bath tonight after dinner, then hang them up to dry. I can iron them after school, so they should be ready to print after dinner on Wednesday."

"What does the alum do?" I ask.

"It helps the fabric retain the print, so it doesn't wash off when I rinse the fabric to remove the size from the carrageenan marbling bath," replies JZ.

"I can't wait to try it," I say. "Hey, is there a grocery

store around here? I need a couple things for my volcano project."

"The Piggly Wiggly is just around the corner," says Gigi.

"Perfect! I need a plastic tablecloth," I say.

Chapter 27
Volcano Prep

It's 4:30 by the time I get home. Mom is planning dinner for 6, so I have time to start on my volcano before dinner. I watch a couple kayaks in the lagoon as I set up to work on the deck.

I have two goals for this evening: *one*–do a test of the colored flame and figure out how to suspend it over the glass vase, *two*–start the work on the papier-mâché volcano construction.

I set up my *eye*Pad on the deck and fire it up. I know the recipe for papier-mâché paste, but it's an excuse to chat with Sam, and talking to a tablet won't raise eyebrows. I ask her to research some more flame effects while I work on the papier-mâché base.

I grab some bubble wrap, styrofoam, clear plastic packing tape, duct tape, cardboard, scissors, and the green plastic tablecloth I bought at the Piggly Wiggly.

First, I cover the piece of plywood with the green plastic table cloth, wrapping it like a Christmas present, trimming the excess material away. I tape the ends securely with the clear packing tape. I don't want my base to get soaked.

Next, I take a cardboard box that's long enough on one side to cover the vase, and I cut off one side of the end tabs. I cut it open and re-bend the long sides to form a rough circle around the vase. Then I make cuts into the end flaps on the remaining end, kind of like you'd clip a curve in sewing a seam, so that you can turn it. This lets the end tabs fan out on the base.

That prep done, I wrap the box back around the vase, overlapping the cardboard loosely. I tape it in place with a couple pieces of tape, one at the top and one at the bottom.

I center it on the base, spread the end flaps outwards. I check that I can get the vase in and out okay. Once I'm happy with the fit around the vase, I tape the end tabs in place on the base. This will provide a central support for my papier-mâché.

I cut a chunk of the styrofoam for a base to hold my Romanesco on toothpicks, and use duct tape to secure that in place. This area will be my forest.

Next, I twist pieces of bubble wrap to form the slopes of my mountain, securing them in place with clear packing tape. I carefully avoid taping over my styrofoam section. That's about it.

Now it's time for the papier-mâché. This is the fun part. I take the newspapers and tear them into long strips. Next, I grab a large bowl and mix some flour and warm water together for the paste. I dip one strip of newspaper after another into the flour and water paste, using my fingers to squeegee out the excess water and arrange them on my structure to shape the sides of my volcano.

As I work, Sam asks me about how my sit-upon design worked out.

"So what did you like best about your design?" Sam asks.

"It was really light, and I liked having the tarp. It gave me room to work." I say.

"Anything you didn't like?" asks Sam. "Or any extra features you'd like?"

"Well, Sue had a nice-sized, fabric-covered kneeling pad. I kind of wish I could open mine out and maybe not need a tarp. And I'd like a better shoulder strap. Something I could wear across my body. So it doesn't fall off my shoulder so easily."

"So what are you thinking for round two?" asks Sam.

"Actually… I was kind of thinking of a folding sit-upon, and skip the tarp. The plastic trash bag stuck to my legs a bit. And maybe use magnets to snap the ends together when it's folded up."

"Hmm… I like it," smiles Sam. "You're really getting the hang of this rapid prototyping stuff."

An hour later, I'm ready to take a break and let my handiwork dry. My volcano is starting to take shape. I'll need to finish the shaping tomorrow, so I'll have time to paint it Thursday.

The flame test will have to wait until after dinner.

Chapter 28
Dinner-Choices

MOM CALLS US inside for dinner. Chicken quinoa casserole with a spinach salad. Talk at dinner centers on the house-hunting progress.

"We looked at four villas today," Dad starts. "Here's the deal—everything in our price range is either two or three bedrooms. Queens Grant has one 3B/2.5 bath villa and a few large 2B/2B villas that could be converted to 3B/3B, like Aunt Gertrude's. It would take a couple months to do the conversion, but we'd get to make the choices."

"I think we all like the location here," Mom continues. "But a three-bedroom villa means Logan and Archer share a room, and being short on storage space and project space. We won't have a garage or a basement like we did in Kodiak."

"If we got a conversion like Aunt Gertrude's place here, could Archer and I have the upstairs suite?" Logan asks.

"You and Logan would get first dibs on the bedroom—other than the master bedroom," Dad confirms.

"Well, we'd probably have more space with an upstairs suite here than we did with two separate bedrooms in Kodiak. Those rooms were tiny," says Archer.

"We won't have a garage. Could we add a storage area to the deck or patio area to shelter our bikes?" says Logan. "Or could I bring it inside?" His bike is the only expensive one, having saved carefully over the years for his bike upgrades.

"Not to rain on your parade, but the finances will be trickier to buy a 2B/2B and then shell out for the conversion, which costs around $50,000. We have to research all the costs, including insurance, condo fees, plantation association fees, and property taxes. There's fewer hidden expenses when you rent, so renting will probably be our default option," says Dad.

"I know we would all like to stay on Hilton Head. You've already started schools here, and the island has a lot to offer. The trees and the shade here really make a difference biking around. The suburbs of Savannah that we looked at were treeless by comparison. We're going to look at some other options around the island tomorrow," says Mom. "I just don't think a villa's going to have enough space for us."

Chapter 29
Sit-Upon V2

As everyone heads out onto the deck, I head upstairs, dragging my feet. I see Sam scurry along the beams and dart under the door into the second floor bedroom suite. She's on the table next to my air mattress, waiting for me when I open the door.

"So, what's really on your mind?" she says as I enter the room and collapse on the mattress.

"Part of me likes it here and really wants to stay," I admit.

"Most people would jump at a chance to live by such a nice beach," Sam prompts.

"I love being near the beach, of course. And the lagoons are super-cool. But even better than that have been the friends I've made—Gigi, JZ, Margot, Jim, and Jenn. They don't seem to mind how weird or klutzy I am at times. They've been so wonderful. And I like the teachers, too. Who else gets to do design projects in art class?"

"But…" Sam prompts.

"SW. Sue Wexford. Super Witch. I just want to

crawl under a rock when she looks my way. It's been one thing after another with her from the first day," I admit. "Of course, part of that is my fault. Super-klutz. She's told the whole school that I'm wearing her cast-off clothes by now. But her friend Lynne didn't have to dump tomato soup on me at lunch today. That hurt."

"Would you like me to turn her into a snake?" Sam asks.

"What? Can you do that?" I gasp, startled. I don't really know what Sam's limits are. Suddenly I turn pale. What if she could? What if she did? Things could get a lot worse.

Sam is still watching me. I see her nod her head as she watches my reaction to her offer.

"No, please don't do anything to Sue or Lynne," I say. It seems important to be clear.

"I couldn't do that anyway," admits Sam. "At least, I don't think so. Is she really so bad that you would want to leave school here? Isn't there anything else worth staying for?"

Several faces pop back into my mind. Gigi. JZ. Margot. Jim. I have already found friends here. Good friends. Suddenly one spoiled rich kid and my eternal humiliation don't seem to matter so much.

It finally dawns on me. My real problem isn't Sue. It's not her fault I'm a klutz. And it's not like I can escape myself and take only the best parts of me wherever I go. Maybe I have to go a little easier on myself… and others. Learn to laugh at myself. Not take things so personally. Okay, one step at a time.

Noticing my transformation, Sam nods her head again, satisfied, then asks, "Is there anything else I can help you with?"

"Not unless you can turn a 3B/3B villa into Dr. Who's TARDIS... you know, bigger on the inside than the outside," I say, sighing.

"No, I can't quite mess with time and relative dimensions in space, yet. That's a bit above my pay-grade. Maybe in the next lifetime, though," quips Sam.

But she's done it. Somehow, my heart is just a little bit lighter. I may not have a plan for staying in Palmetto Dunes yet, but I'm motivated and have a clear goal. And I think I have an ally in Aunt Gertrude. Maybe even Logan and Archer.

I settle down on my air mattress, sketching out my ideas for a sit-upon revision. Then I gather the materials I need and get to work on my second prototype. This time I go all out, and use a pretty Caribbean blue marine grade fabric. I have a yard of the material at 60 inches wide, and I only need a piece 30 inches by 30 inches for my design. That leaves me a 30 by 36-inch piece for future projects along with a 6-inch by 30-inch remnant... just about an ideal size for making some zippered pencil pouches.

I even make a zippered pocket using patterning scrim—a clear plastic material with white reinforcing fibers running on a diamond pattern. Lightweight and waterproof, plus you can see what's inside. And it's a lot cheaper than the blue fabric.

I attach D-rings to hold a shoulder strap, one on each end, plus one in the middle, so when I fold it, I still have a D-ring on the folded side for the shoulder strap.

The magnets are a bit trickier than I thought. The super magnets may be super-strong, but they don't work through the thick blue fabric. So I improvise and make thin fabric tubes from a thin black ripstop material. I cut the tube into six pieces, which I make into tabs. Three go on each outer edge of the sit-upon. I'm careful to insert the magnets so that the poles match up when I fold the sit-upon, then re-sew the side seams with the magnetic tabs in place. And it works! The magnets are strong enough through the thin ripstop.

This time I use two Amazon bubble-wrap envelopes for the padding. They're stiffer and lighter than the four layers of the pink bubble wrap I used for my first prototype. And this prototype is heavier, about 12.5 ounces compared with just 7 ounces for my first try. Still under a pound though.

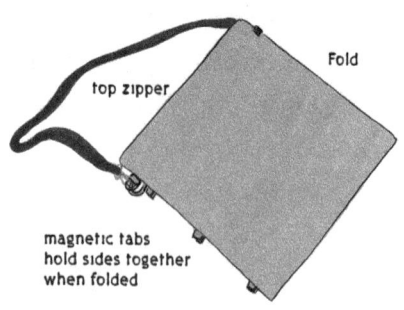

It's not as cute as my first prototype, but the design is more ingenious. Not a bad effort for a future inventor, I think. I can't wait to try it out tomorrow.

Chapter 30

Flame Test

I ROLL OUT of bed, remembering that I didn't have time to do my flame tests last night. I check the volcano. The papier-mâché is dry. I'll need to build up another layer after school.

The house is still quiet. Time to do a quick flame test before breakfast, I think.

I gather Sam, some rubbing alcohol, matches, a glass bowl, table salt, and Epsom salts and head out onto the deck. I hear Curie racing along the floor in the great room. Not sure what she's playing with, but it's not Sam.

First, I take the table salt, placing some in the bottom of the bowl. Then I pour in a little rubbing alcohol, wait a minute, light a match, and set the rubbing alcohol on fire, careful to blow out the match before setting it down. The flame burns brightly, but I don't notice any special colored effects. After a minute, the flame has burned off all the rubbing alcohol and dies out.

I repeat the experiment, this time using Epsom

salts. Magnesium is supposed to give off a bright white light. Instead, I see the same yellow orange flames. Normal-looking flames to me.

A thought occurs to me, and this time I use only rubbing alcohol. No salts. The flame looks the same. I guess that's just what rubbing alcohol looks like when you burn it.

I recheck my notes. Magnesium burns bright white, sodium burns yellow, and strontium burns red. I still have the strontium chloride that Sam made, but I feel awkward about using it. Sighing, I decide that I may as well test it. I can decide later.

I take about half my sample and put it in the glass bowl, adding the rubbing alcohol, and light it with a match. The top of the flame is still orange yellow, but a beautiful red color flashes across the base of the bowl as the strontium chloride burns. It's a nice effect. But should I use it?

Is it an unfair advantage? Instant printing of whatever you want… I think that might qualify as unfair. Although, anyone can buy this on Amazon, I rationalize. *I* still have time to buy this on Amazon. Anyway, couldn't unlimited wealth be considered an unfair advantage?

Satisfied with my flame test, I turn to clean up my mess when I suddenly notice the bowl has a smoky haze to it. Crap! I should have used aluminum foil. Maybe it's payback for thinking about a shortcut.

I rush into the kitchen and start working to scour

the bowl clean. Dawn dishwashing detergent doesn't do it. I hear movement in the bedrooms as the rest of the house starts to wake, so I shove the bowl in the dishwasher. Maybe the dishwasher can get it clean.

As I head back to the stairs, I see a floppy black blob hanging to the carpet of the lowest step where Curie was a moment ago. I wonder if a wasp got inside somehow. Then I take a closer look. It's not a wasp.

Logan hasn't been using my caterpillars for fish bait.

It's a female black swallowtail butterfly. Ginger. But her wings are bent at weird angles.

Gently, I reach down and put my fingers by her legs. She climbs up onto my hand, and I carry her outside. I go to the table on the deck and try to straighten her wing, but it's hardened. It's not broken, it's permanently bent.

And then it hits me. Curie must have found her while her wings were still soft and played with her. While I was doing my stupid flame test, Curie was playing with Ginger, bending her wings while they were still hardening. But now there's nothing I can do to fix it. She can't fly. She'll never fly.

I do the only thing I can think of. I place her on some flowers so she can drink some nectar. When she gets tired of drinking nectar, I put her on some parsley where she pretends to lay some eggs. Then I put her back on the flowers.

Chapter 31

Round 2

IN SCIENCE CLASS, Mr. DiPilla scores another memorable experiment, demonstrating a chemical sculpture. "Sodium acetate is a liquid that is really just looking for any excuse to turn into a solid," he explains. "In this case, I have a few crystals on this plate." He pours some of the liquid onto the crystals, and it magically transforms into a solid, building up a white irregular column as he pours.

"There's a practical application to this," he continues. "When sodium acetate undergoes the phase transformation from liquid to solid, it gives off heat. It doesn't get above 130 degrees Fahrenheit, and it lasts for a good 30 to 60 minutes, making it a handy heating pad or hand warmer. Some companies manufacture these as a sealed plastic pouch with a small, thin curved metal disk inside. When you press on the disk, bending it, it clicks. That click is enough to start the transformation to solid. The sodium acetate can be reset to the liquid state by putting the pouch into boiling water for 20 minutes. So, you can reuse the heating pads many times."

"Just a word of caution," adds Mr. DiPilla. "We will be doing some chemical experiments this week. It is very important that you do not try to concoct your own chemical creations without proper supervision and research. Never mix household chemicals without a tested recipe or set of instructions. Some chemical reactions give off toxic fumes. For example, many household cleaners have ammonia or chlorine bleach as an ingredient. If you mix ammonia and bleach together, you may not live to tell about it."

I HEAD INTO ART CLASS, toting my backpack and my latest prototype to find the rest of the class gathered around Sue Wexford… who is proudly displaying her Tommy Bahama backpack beach chair. It's kind of the ultimate solution to the sit-upon challenge. Two zipper pockets on the back, including one insulated pocket for beverages. Plus cup-holders and arm-rests. And it all folds up so you can carry it on your back.

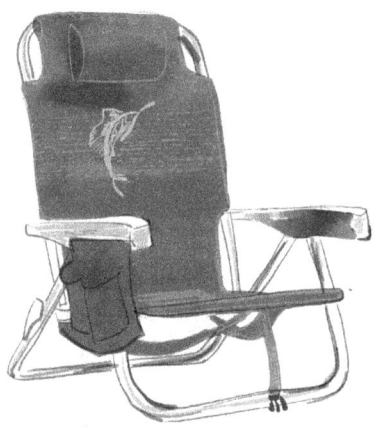

Sue catches my eye and gives me a superior smile. She thinks she's nailed it.

"That's thinking outside the box," compliments Mr. Shelley. "What inspired you to think of a beach chair?"

"Well, I thought about the things I wish my sit-up-on had but didn't, like a pocket to hold my sketch pad. And I wanted something a little more comfortable to sit on. So I tried to think what else we had around the house that would work. And that's when I thought of our beach chairs," says Sue with a smile.

"Does anyone else have something new to share today? A tweak to your first prototypes from yesterday?"

I set my backpack down and raise my hand shakily.

"Yes, Putney," Mr. Shelley says. "What do you have to show us today?"

"I designed a folding sit-upon," I say, holding my prototype up for everyone to see. I show the magnetic tabs and the interior zipper pocket.

"That's a very creative design," says Mr. Shelley. "How did you come up with the idea?"

I take out my *eye*Pad and show the new sketches I made.

"At first, I wanted a larger sit-upon, but it was too huge to carry. So I settled on the smaller sit-upon and tarp idea. But I liked the size of Sue's sit-upon yesterday, and that got me thinking that maybe I could design something that folded in half, so it wouldn't be so huge to carry. And then I thought of magnets to hold it together when folded. I thought maybe this would be big enough so that I wouldn't need a tarp, which would make set-up and clean-up a snap.

"Well done, both of you. This is shaping up to be quite a contest," beams Mr. Shelley. "I think we're going to have to take a class vote on Friday to determine the final winner with bragging rights—but let's take a quick vote now... raise your hand if you like the backpack beach chair best."

I look around. A lot of hands raise in the air. More than half. Sue's solution really is a Cadillac... it has everything you could want. And more.

"Now raise your hand if you like the folding sit-upon best," says Mr. Shelley.

Fewer hands go up this time. JZ, Margot, Gigi, and Jim raise their hands immediately.

"I think we have a few undecided voters we need to persuade," observes Mr. Shelley. "Anyone care to share why they voted for the backpack beach chair?"

Bryce raises his hand and says, "Have you taken a look at this beach chair? It has everything you could want and more. Cooler bag pocket, another zipper pocket big enough for your sketch pad and pencils. Cup holders. Padded backpack straps. Plus, they're super comfortable to sit in."

"Anyone care to share why they voted for the folding sit-upon?" asks Mr. Shelley.

This time Jim raises his hand and says, "I voted for what I thought would work best if I had to use it myself. Have you taken a 15-minute hike with a backpack beach chair? They weigh like 8 to 10 pounds empty. Putney's solution can't weigh more than a pound. But then again, I like traveling light. I don't mind sitting on the ground."

"Great observations, both of you," smiles Mr. Shelley. "Keep that in mind for the final vote on Friday. I encourage you to vote for the option you would most like to use—and carry—yourself. But based on the today's vote, I think we have to declare Miss Wexford the winner of Round Two."

"Okay, time to go back out and do some more sketching. And you can try out your latest prototypes to see how they do in the field. We still have two more days before we declare our final winner."

JZ, Gigi, Margot, and I are the first ones out the door, eager to get to sketching again. Sue and her posse lag behind, which is a good thing because that backpack beach chair is huge. She's got to go through the door sideways! It doesn't look too light either.

We go back to the duck lagoon for a second day of sketching. I set up by the small lagoon again. My solution may not look so elegant, but it's way easier to carry. And I like sitting on the ground to sketch. I hate to admit it, but I kinda miss my tarp. I'd still like more room to spread out. Hmm, still room for improvement I think. But that's an easy fix. After all, I have a 30-inch by 36-inch piece of fabric left from making my sit-upon. Perfect size for a tarp.

The time passes quickly, and when Mr. Shelley gives us the 5-minute warning to pack up, I take my time to do a little more sketching. I know I can pack my stuff up in a snap.

I do sneak a couple peaks as Sue begins the process of stowing her drawing materials and folding her chair back up. It takes her a couple tries to get the legs folded.

We lag behind Sue and her posse as we head back down the golf cart path. Sue is clever. Half the class is still buzzing about her backpack beach chair. She "lets" Bryce take a turn carrying it for her. Behind them, Lynne and Liz—aka ponytail girl—chat with her.

I hang way back with Gigi, JZ, and Margot.

I hate to admit it, but I smirk as I watch Bryce squeeze through the door with the backpack beach chair. Evidently, the "Cadillac" solution does have its downside.

I grab my backpack to head to class, but pause when I sling it over my shoulder. Something doesn't feel right. It takes a second to register that it feels a bit light. Half the class is already out the door by the time I look inside.

My *eye*Pad is missing.

Chapter 32
The Principal's Office Again

"No," I gasp as I start pulling things out of my backpack.

"What's wrong?" asks Gigi as she hurries to my side.

"My *eye*Pad is missing," I say as Mr. Shelley comes up beside us.

"You locked the room again, right?" I ask. He nods in reply.

"You sure you brought it to class?" asks Margot.

"Yeah... I showed more sketches, remember?" I say.

"Check the pockets again," Mr. Shelley instructs. "Make sure you didn't put it in a different pocket or something."

I hold out the empty backpack to him and let him search for himself. It's not there. On the table are a couple notepads and my math book for next period, and a pencil pouch.

"If your iPad isn't in your backpack, then someone must have removed it and stashed it somewhere. But how? Where?" says Margot.

"And when?" adds JZ. "We were first out of the room.

So there might have been time as we were leaving."

"Yeah," adds Margot. "And Sue's backpack thing would have been the perfect screen for someone to hide behind as they snatched it. Maybe even a great place to stow it while it was smuggled out of the room."

"We don't know that it was removed from this room yet," says Mr. Shelley. "And I would advise you to be careful about accusing Miss Wexford of anything. She's not the type to pull a prank like this."

"Almost any of the sit-upons would be large enough to hold it," says Gigi.

"Except the ones that were duct-taped shut like mine wouldn't work," adds JZ.

"The real question is, where is it now? And how will I ever get it back?" I moan.

We look under the tables as Mr. Shelley searches the shelves and the desk drawers. It does not appear to be in the room.

"We'll need to make a report to the principal," he says. "Come with me."

WE HEAD to the administration offices off the main hallway next to the Multi-Purpose Room, but Mr. Hauck isn't there. Mrs. Roberts, the counselor, explains that he is at a meeting at Hilton Head Middle School on the north end of the island, but is expected back after lunch.

Mr. Shelley explains the situation, sticking to the

simple facts.

"Her iPad appears to have been removed from her backpack in art class, either as we were leaving to sketch or after we returned," says Mr. Shelley. "We searched the classroom and didn't find it. And she got it out at the beginning of class to show her design sketches. So it *was* in the classroom."

"Can you describe the make and model of the iPad?" asks Mrs. Roberts.

"Uh, it was a gift. I just got it on Sunday. It didn't come in an Apple box, so I'm not sure about the exact model. But it's the classic size. And it came in a grey case," I stammer as I realize I don't have a good way to describe it, or even have any proof of purchase.

"Do you have a record of the serial number somewhere?" Mrs. Roberts prompts.

"No… maybe Miss Pepper does. She's the person who gave it to me," I say with a sinking feeling. I don't even have any photos of it. And Sam! Where is she?

"Did you register it with the "Find My iPad" feature?" she asks.

I try to remember everything Sam guided me through that first evening. "I'm set up with an Apple ID, so maybe. But I don't have a cellular plan for it," I say. It's just super-sneaky about connecting to networks. But I don't say that out loud, because I don't know the school's WIFI password. I think that's only for teachers.

"Surely this is a spur-of-the-moment prank," says

Mrs. Roberts. "Doesn't your iPad have a security passcode? And even if they get through the passcode, the first time they connect to a network we should be able to use the 'Find My iPad' app to locate it. There's not much a 12-year-old can do with a stolen iPad."

"I think Mrs. Roberts is right," says Mr. Shelley.

"Is there anything we can do right now?" I ask.

"If our main goal is to get it back, we should make it easy for it to be found and returned. Perhaps an announcement asking for help locating it and asking for it to be handed in to the Administration Office," says Mrs. Roberts. "I'll talk to Principal Hauck when he returns. I suggest you return to class and try not to worry."

Chapter 33

The Search

WE FILE INTO math class, searching for seats near the back. Everyone else is already seated, books out. There are only four seats left in the front row. Great.

As I make my way to an empty seat, I glance around. Lots of kids have their backpacks with them. Then it hits me… what I don't see. Sue's backpack beach chair. It's not here. Where is it? It's too big to fit in a locker. So where is she keeping it?

Mr. Geiger forces me to pay attention. Downside of sitting in the front row. Or upside, I guess, depending on your point of view. Or at least it forces me to give the appearance of paying attention.

WE SWING by our lockers after math class on the way to the cafeteria. No point in swinging by the principal's office until the end of lunch period. We're all bursting with questions.

"When did they take it?"
"How did they smuggle it out?"
"Where is it now?"

"Who took it?"

We pause, looking at each other. Then I say, "I keep going over it in my head. I think it was grabbed on the way out of art class to go sketch. We were in front of everybody. Sue and her friends were last out of the room."

"I don't think Sue would steal anything," says Gigi. "I think Mrs. Roberts is right about it being a prank."

"Maybe. But that backpack chair of hers would have been the perfect thing to smuggle it out of class with," says Margot.

"But Sue's not the only one who handled that chair. Everyone was gathered around it. Bryce carried it for her on the way back to class," points out Gigi.

"But that's what I've been wondering. Where is Sue's chair now? It's too big to fit in her locker, so where does she have it stashed?" I say.

JZ shakes her head. "Even if Sue did this, she'd be stupid to leave it in her beach chair. That's like leaving a smoking gun in your own locker. So either it's stashed some place in or close to the school, or on the way to the lagoon where we sketched."

"Why take it?" I ask. "She's got better stuff than I do."

"Again, you're assuming Sue took it," says Gigi.

"Well, yeah. This feels personal," I say.

"Don't matter who took it. If we want to find it, I want to know how they stashed it," says JZ.

"You're devious," says Margot, "and creative. If you were going to snatch it, where would you stash it?"

JZ smiles as she considers this. "Well, first I'd need a diversion to get it out of Putney's backpack."

"All the commotion around Sue's beach chair as she left the room would be perfect. It's so big, it'd make a perfect screen," adds Margot.

"Okay, so now you've got the *eye*Pad," I say. "Easy enough to hide it under your own sketchbook or sit-upon as you exit the classroom. What next?"

"Well, there's really three options after you leave the art room: go straight out the main door with the rest of us, turn right and go out the side door by the art room, or go left past the lockers towards the cafeteria and possibly out the entrance by the cafeteria."

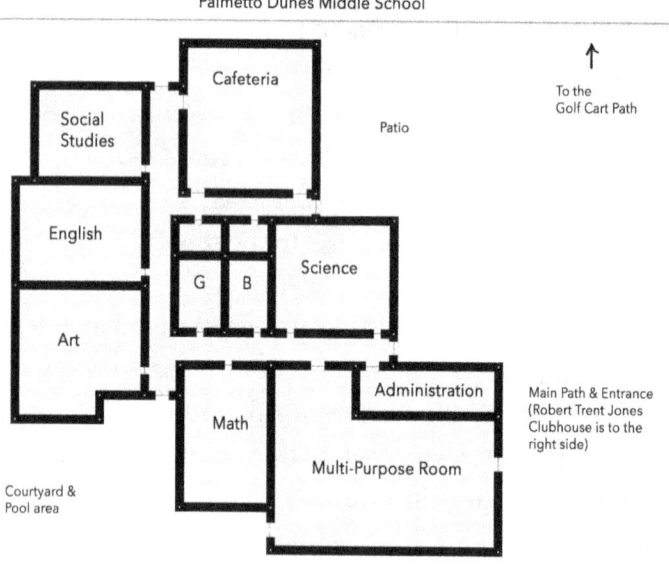

"Mr. Shelley brought up the rear today, so I'm thinking it'd be harder to stash something going straight out the main entrance. Plus, we were last coming back, and we'd have seen if someone stashed something on the way back," I say.

"So what do you think, JZ?" asks Gigi. "Stash it in a locker to the left, or outside to the right?"

"If it were me?" clarifies JZ. "I wouldn't put it in my locker. You'd be asking for trouble if someone searched and found it there."

"So you'd stash it outside?" I ask. "What about dirt and rain and being seen? How would you grab it later?"

"First off, it's not my iPad, and it's a heist, so I wouldn't be picky about dirt and stuff. Plus the pine needle mulch around the palms and shrubs would keep it pretty clean. Maybe even help hide it. And the big palmetto leaves would make a pretty good cover for hiding something. Plus, there are tons of places under the decking where something could be stashed," answers JZ.

"And we're allowed to go outside for lunch... crap," says Gigi. "We should be outside right now."

"Yeah, but if they took it out during lunch, doesn't that mean it's not a one-person job?" I say.

JZ looks grim as she says, "There's a difference between agreeing to something like this up front, and ratting out a friend who pulls a stupid prank on a lark."

Margot nods her head in agreement, "Sue may not have planned for this to happen, but I bet she knows about it now."

"So, what are we waiting for, let's go," I say. Another thought crosses my mind. If I can get close enough, maybe Sam can find *me*. What's bluetooth range? About 10 feet? Fifteen? Twenty?

We head out the door by the cafeteria and walk around to the front corner of the building to start our search. As we glance around, there's still a bunch of students sitting on a deck in front which wraps around a group of palm trees. It's really just a platform with no rails and sits about a foot off the ground. The sides are about 6 inches high, leaving about a 6-inch gap underneath. Perfect for stashing something.

I don't see Sue anywhere. But I see ponytail-girl on her own, heading inside the side door closest to the art room.

We fan out. JZ and Margot search the plants next to the building. Gigi and I head towards the deck. I keep my eyes on the ground, searching for Sam. We only have about 5 minutes left for lunch. I head for the empty side of the deck, and that's when I feel something land on my shoulder.

Chapter 34
Choices

I TRIP AND FALL, landing on my hands and knees.

A voice hisses in my ear, "About time you found me. I was worried about how I'd reach you in time. I think one of them would have taken me home."

I release the breath I'd been holding, my mind flashing with possibilities as Gigi comes up beside me. But now's not the time to question Sam.

"Are you okay?" Gigi asks, coming up beside me.

"Yeah, super-klutz strikes again. Must've tripped over a root or something," I say. "I thought this would be a good place to start. Wish I had a flashlight."

"It'd probably be within arms reach, so we just need to pat down the mulch underneath the deck on each side, right?" says Gigi.

Some of the other students stare at us as we search. I'm just about to the end of the first side when my fingers touch a familiar surface.

"You found it," confirms Sam in my ear. I feel the pressure leave my shoulder as she jumps off and scuttles underneath the deck.

I pull it out and show Gigi. "Got it!" I say, relief flooding over me.

JZ and Margot hurry over.

"Thank you guys so much for helping me figure this out. We did it! We solved the mystery," I say.

"We still don't know who took it," says JZ. "So, you've got a choice. Put it back and try to catch them when they come back for it. Or keep it and report back to Mrs. Roberts and the principal."

"I'm not letting it out of my sight again," I say. "Anyway—what if they saw us find it? They'll know it's a trap. I just want this drama to be over."

WE HEAD BACK to the administration office. Mr. Shelly is inside with Mrs. Roberts and Mr. Hauck. I hold out the *eye*Pad and explain how JZ figured out where to look, and where we found it.

"Did you see anyone near where you found it?" Mr. Shelley asks.

"By the time we thought to look there, there were only a couple groups of kids on two of the other sides of the deck," I say.

Gigi hesitates, then says, "I saw Liz Ogelthorpe heading inside as we reached the deck. She was on her own."

Mr. Hauck exchanges a look with Mrs. Roberts.

"May I hold onto this for the rest of the day?" Mr. Hauck asks. "I wouldn't want anything else unfortunate to happen to it, say during gym class. You can pick it up here at the end of the day."

"Uh, sure," I say. "Thank you."

It probably is the safest option. Not like it'd be safe to talk to Sam until we get home, anyway.

IN GYM CLASS, Mr. McCabe teaches us a few new maneuvers, a pincer movement, and the end-around, which Brock introduced us to yesterday.

This time, Mr. McCabe instructs both teams to try to keep possession of the puck. It really helps the team defending the deep end to learn to work as a team.

The pincer movement is a two-on-one maneuver designed to squeeze the person with the puck to make it easier to steal the puck.

I still mess up on positioning, but my teamwork is improving as I look for my teammates and observe the positioning. Now that I'm not just trying to score, I'm actually able to help maintain possession of the puck.

Jim compliments me on my progress.

I feel bad when I mess up, but everyone is supportive and constructive in breaking down the points, and pointing out what we could have done differently. I'm starting to understand teamwork through underwater hockey. Who knew?

And it helps me put the whole *eye*Pad thing behind me.

Chapter 35

Marbling

AFTER SCHOOL is dismissed, I come home and finish my papier-mâché volcano construction, taking breaks to move Ginger between the flowers and the parsley. Curie watches, but Ginger's out of reach.

While working, I ask Sam what she knows about the heist from this morning.

"All I know is that someone lifted me out of your backpack and put me under the deck where you found me. I don't really know who took me—I was in sleep mode. All I know is that it wasn't you when someone powered me on," says Sam. "I scanned them. Then I said, 'You're not Putney. Who are you?' and I was dropped. Then a girl said, 'Try searching for her sketches.' And a boy said, 'No way. That's not a normal iPad. That's crazy security. I'm getting out of here.' And that's about it. Someone shoved me back under the deck, then I took Emergency Lizard Form, scooted out, and climbed the palm tree where you found me. Or I found you."

"So, did you see anything?" I say.

"Well, I don't know who they are," says Sam. "By the time I took lizard form and could look around, I only saw a boy and a girl walking into the school while another group of kids came out carrying lunch bags."

"Can you describe them?" I ask.

"They both had blond hair," Sam says.

"Long hair? Short hair? Ponytail? Curly? Straight?" I prompt.

"No ponytail. Hair was too short to pull back like that. But not curly either. More of a short bob," says Sam.

Sue and Bryce, I think. But where were Lynne and Liz? Maybe it was a prank that got out of hand, and only Sue was curious enough to check further because of the bet?

Sam studies me. "Let it go," she advises. "You can't prove anything. But next time, try pinging me with the Find My iPad app. I just have to find a valid WIFI network, then you can get Mr. Hauck to pinpoint my location."

"Well, I'm leaving you home tomorrow. So maybe there won't be a next time," I say.

"Or just keep me with you," counters Sam.

"I wish you were more portable," I muse.

MOM COMES outside to check on me, and I remember the smoky glass bowl in the dishwasher. So I offer to unload the dishwasher with dishes from breakfast and lunch, and then set the table for dinner. The glass bowl still has a smoky hue. I try scrubbing it again and put it back in the dishwasher. Maybe a second pass will work.

For my sit-upon version 3 prototype, I take the 30-inch by 36-inch fabric remnant and fold it in thirds each way. The resulting 10-inch by 12-inch rectangle fits neatly into a pocket of my sit-upon. Mission accomplished. It is a bit heavier, about 1.3 pounds now. But nowhere near as heavy as Sue's backpack beach chair.

DISCUSSION AT DINNER focuses on the house-hunting process.

"We looked at a few houses in Hilton Head Plantation today," Dad says. "There are a few within our budget that have four bedrooms. Problem is, we can't do short-term rentals there. So, it wouldn't be ideal for us to rent out when we're transferred next."

"And it's not so convenient to the beach or stores. We've been spoiled here with this location. Palmetto Dunes is my favorite plantation. I just don't think we can make a villa work long-term. We'd just be so tight on space," Mom says, then sighs. "Unless someone has a new idea, I think we're going to have to rent a house in Savannah."

AFTER DINNER, we take a walk on the beach. A group of people are playing boules in the sand. Either that or bocce ball. I can't really tell the difference. A golden retriever dances in the waves, retrieving a floating toy. A family cycles down the beach on a bicycle made for two. You see all kinds of bikes here.

All I can think of is how much I'll miss the beach and my new friends here on Hilton Head. Savannah may be a cool city, but a suburb's a suburb. It's not special like here.

I check my watch, then head over to JZ's villa in Hickory Cove. It's a two-story townhouse with a deck that backs onto part of the big lagoon that makes one of several loops in Palmetto Dunes. We head out back onto her deck and she shows me how to marble fabric.

"Marbling is relaxing. And fun. Let go of that drama today," she quips.

A large plastic bin rests on the floor of the deck, filled with a cream-colored slimy liquid.

First, she splatters various drops of dyes on the surface. Then she takes a long metal comb, and rakes the surface in one continuous motion, forming an intricate pattern. It reminds me of the icing glaze on a fancy pastry that Aunt Gertrude buys at the Hilton Head Social Bakery—Napoleon's. Then she takes a single metal stylus, and, starting in the center, makes a spiral motion. This forms the classic James Bond gun barrel look from the title sequences of the movies.

I marvel at how the colors are pulled along by the metal pins, making intricate patterns. I wonder what the science behind it is. Yeah, science geek. That's me. Right brain creates, left brain analyzes.

Now we're ready to lay the treated fabric on the

marbling bath. We each take two corners and gently lower the fabric onto the bath, touching down in the center first. As soon as the fabric is completely down, JZ picks it up and dips it in a bucket of water.

"That's to rinse the carrageenan size out of it," she explains as she hangs it on a drying rack.

We do a few more, then it's my turn to try. This is so cool. I love watching how the stylus pulls the color along with it, forming intricate patterns on the top of the carrageenan.

By the time we finish, not quite an hour later, we've printed 50 napkins, and eight are for me. They'll make a special present for Aunt Gertrude. I made four in aqua tones and four in peach tones. JZ tells me she'll bring mine to school after they've dried and she's had a chance to iron them to set the dyes.

Here's a photo of one of the test napkins, printed in high contrast purple and pink tones. Pretty cool, huh?

Chapter 36
Problem Solving

JZ WALKS part of the way with me as I head home. I look around, thinking about our housing options as I walk past expensive homes and villas. The closer you are to the ocean, the more expensive the property. JZ is pretty close to the beach, plus she has lagoon access right there. It's a sweet location, and yet I think I prefer Queens Grant. The duck lagoon seems more private and magical somehow. You can get so close to the water. It seems like there's always a special visitor around… anhinga, egret, or heron.

"Cat got your tongue?" JZ asks. "You seem really quiet. Still thinking about the heist?"

"No, it's not that. It's just…" I let out a deep breath and everything starts spilling out. I explain about the rental homes in Savannah, the perceived shortcomings of the villa options. "I really really want to stay here on the island, and I love Queens Grant. We're managing camping out with Aunt Gertrude because our stuff is still on a container somewhere between Alaska and here. Mom just doesn't think we can make a villa work, even if Logan and Archer double up and share a bedroom," I say.

"What's the biggest problem, do you think?" prods JZ. "What *kind* of space are you short on?"

"Well, the kitchen's a good size except for the refrigerator. We're a big family, so a larger refrigerator would be helpful. Maybe a freezer too," I hedge.

"What else?" prompts JZ. "What about your dad?"

"Dad's always had an office—a place to work on projects on the computer, make things, and work out. He also sews, making things like back packs, waterproof iPad cases, and gun holsters, but that can be done on a portable folding table. In Kodiak, you don't go hiking without protection from bears."

"Hmm… a man cave," interprets JZ. "What about your mom?"

"Mom paints when she has time and does stuff on the computer. But she's more portable, making use of small nooks, and cleaning up after a painting session. And she's so creative. She will figure out the best use of every square inch of space. She'll figure out something for Dad, although it might not be ideal…" I trail off as a thought hits me.

JZ seems to notice. "What is it?" she asks. "You have that look… like you've just figured something out."

"I think what we're *really* missing is messy space—like a basement or garage—or an attic." I think back to my scavenger hunt in the attic and an idea hits me. "What if we could find a way to make the unused attic space more functional? And how much would it cost? That's what we're short of."

"Now you're cooking," says JZ. "My mom's an architect, and I've seen some of the work she does. Most attics don't have a floor, but that's pretty easy to add. Around here, the heat's the killer. You'd probably want to look at air conditioning the space, maybe add insulation and light."

"Any idea how much that would cost?" I ask.

"Not really. But if it doesn't need to be pretty, your dad and brothers may be able to do much of the work themselves. For some things you'll need permits though," JZ muses. "First thing though is to figure out if there's enough space there to be worth it."

"So, I need to do a layout or floor plan," I say.

"You got it," affirms JZ.

"I can do that," I say. "Thanks so much! And thanks for the marbling lesson and napkins."

We part at the bridge, and I turn the corner by the tennis courts, then cut back along the golf cart path towards Aunt Gertrude's villa.

Sam will be able to help me with the floor plans, I think as I round the corner past the duck lagoon and head into the Green. Everyone's sitting outside on the deck as I run inside Aunt Gertrude's villa and run upstairs.

Chapter 37

Attic Possibilities

Sam follows me into the room, and I close the door, breathless from running.

"What's up?" asks Sam, watching me carefully. "You've got a plan, don't you?"

"Yes, but I need to do a layout of the villa to see if it's a good enough plan to make a difference. Can you help me?"

"Easy-peasy," says Sam. "What's the plan?"

I give Sam the short version of the plan… to figure out how much space we could *maybe* gain by making the attic useable. It doesn't mean we don't have to look at the rest of the villa, but Mom will be on top of that. We just have to tip the scales a bit to get Mom and Dad to give this another chance. If a villa like Aunt Gertrude's is what we can afford, we just have to get creative with how to make space like this work.

Which means taking a second look at the attic.

Wood trusses support the villa roof, which forms a peak like the letter "A." As I stand at the entry door to the attic, the cathedral ceiling of the great room forms the left side of the "A," while the attic ceiling forms the right half of the letter "A," slanting from the top of the left-side wall down to the floor on the right side, something like this:

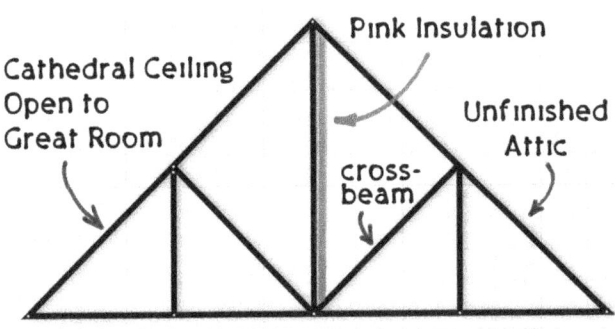

Sketch of Queens Grant Attic Trusses

HALFWAY TO THE RIGHT, vertical beams come up from the floor at about 4-foot intervals. Cross beams come up from the floor by the left wall to join them. It's these cross beams, which slant at about a 45-degree angle, that pose the real problem. I know that you can't cut any additional cross-beams, which is why everyone's been ignoring the attic.

My idea is to make use of the space *between* the cross-beams, as well as the low ceiling space at the ends. Surely there's a lot we could do with this space.

Sam guides me through a couple apps, and before I know it, we have a floor plan of the main floor and second floor, showing the location of the cross-beams in the attic, as well as the heating, ventilation and air-conditioning, or HVAC, system and hot water heater.

Here's the floor plan of the second floor:

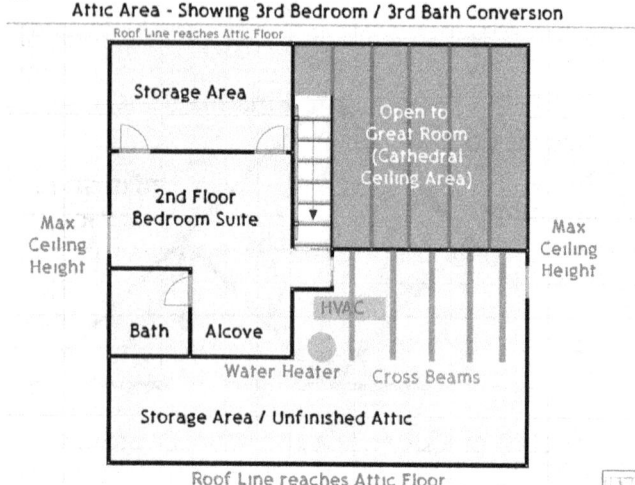

Here's the floor plan of the first floor:

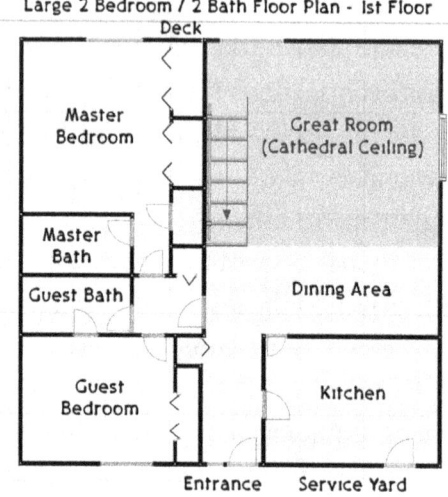

IT'S NOT PERFECT space, but with a bit of work, maybe it will be enough to tip the balance. With the first draft layouts completed, I head downstairs to join the others, *eye*Pad in hand.

LOGAN AND ARCHER sit at the table working on their homework. I settle down on one of the wood benches surrounding the deck, and Sam scuttles up a railing to watch me as I make notes using the Apple Pencil in Adobe Sketch. We all like being outside, enjoying the quiet of the lagoon. Lightning bugs start to come out, flashing around us with the dancing lights of summer as the sun starts to set.

I think my idea for the attic is going to work. I just don't know how expensive it will be. Certainly not as expensive as the 3B/3B conversion. I keep drawing on my *eye*Pad as the night continues to darken. Deck lights provide enough light to work by.

It's dark by the time Mom calls me to get ready for bed. I reluctantly pack up my things and move my volcano inside for the night.

As I head upstairs to bed, I think about what else I can use to clean that glass bowl. Hydrogen peroxide, maybe? Remembering Mr. DiPilla's warning, I ask Sam to research hydrogen peroxide cleaners, then I drift off to sleep.

Chapter 38

Toothpaste

I WAKE UP SUDDENLY... toothpaste! Hydrogen peroxide and baking soda! It could work. I whisper my idea to Sam, as I gather my things together quietly. She crawls up onto my shoulder and whispers back in my ear. "It's a safe cleaning solution, and used for toothpaste, cleaning tile grout, and many other things. You can also mix it with vinegar if that's not strong enough."

I hurry downstairs and dig out the smoky glass bowl. I clean it again using hot soapy water, then try adding hydrogen peroxide and baking soda. I rub the mixture into the sides of the bowl with a paper towel, and the paper towel comes away with some black smudges on it. It's working!

Relief floods me as I repeat this a couple more times until the bowl is clear of the smoky residue. Success!

I run back upstairs to grab my attic sketches. I have a really good feeling about this.

That's when I notice one of my monarch caterpillars is missing.

"Sam, can you help me find my caterpillar? I don't want Curie to get to this one," I whisper.

We search frantically for 5 minutes before Sam points to a caterpillar hanging in a "J" position from the underside of a leaf of a scented geranium plant under the window.

I'm going to have to do a better job tracking my butterfly caterpillars.

And I need to keep Curie out of this room.

I SHARE MY IDEA over breakfast, explaining how we could use the space between the crossbeams and maybe get the project space and additional storage area we were missing.

"I like it," says Dad simply. "This could be a game-changer."

"Just raising the floor and putting in a solid floor would help a lot. But to make it really useful, we'd need to air condition it and maybe put in a window, plus additional electrical outlets and lighting."

"We'd have to draw up some plans and talk to a contractor. I don't know how much that would cost, but nothing like a full conversion that cuts beams and adds a bathroom," muses Dad. "HVAC will be the tricky part, so that's probably the best place to start."

"Don't get your hopes up too much," advises Mom. "This isn't a slam dunk. But it's a really good thought. Meanwhile, I can work on some room layouts, see what we can do there."

"Oh, by the way… I have a monarch caterpillar getting ready to pupate upstairs. Can you help me keep Curie out of our room? I don't want another butterfly ending up with bent wings," I say.

Logan and Archer shake their heads at me.

"Hey, you're Curie's favorite," Archer says. "Not me."

"Yeah," Logan adds. "You gonna kick her off your pillow at night?"

"Well, it's either that or… I guess I could move the scented geranium when Curie's around," I say slowly. And for now, I have another option.

Chapter 39
Round 3

I AM CAUTIOUSLY OPTIMISTIC as I head to school. I left Sam at home, after much grumbling on her part. But she agreed to stay and play with Curie and occasionally slip under the door to the upstairs bedroom to check on the monarch.

When the bell rings at the end of science class, I rush to my locker to get my latest sit-upon prototype and head into art class. After yesterday, I'm anxious to see what Sue has dreamed up this time.

As I enter the room, there's a cluster of students around Sue, looking as she unfolds her latest entry in what has become the sit-upon design challenge. But this time, the boy with spiky blond hair looks up when he sees me enter the room and comes over to *me*.

"Hey, I'm Bryce," he says to me. "So you still got that crazy folding sit-upon design? Can I see it?"

I nod my head and pull it out to show him. Somewhere behind me, I feel Sue's eyes glaring at me.

As the bell rings, we take our seats. Mr. Shelley greets us, asking "So, what did you learn from yesterday's prototypes, and did anyone come up with a new prototype today?"

Sue jumps up from her chair, displaying a three-legged chair. "It's called a folding camp stool. The three legs make it stable on any ground, and it only weighs 5 pounds. That's 3 pounds lighter than the backpack beach chair. So, it should be a lot lighter to carry. And it fits in my locker."

I RAISE MY HAND NEXT, pulling out the tarp from my sit-upon. "I liked my folding sit-upon, but wished I still had a bit more room to spread out on the ground. So I used the remnant piece of fabric to make a tarp. It folds up to stow in a pocket. It adds about half a pound of weight, but it's still only 1.3 pounds without my sketch pad."

"Nice work," compliments Mr. Shelley. "Today we're going to head out to the beach to sketch. That will give you some different terrain to deal with in your designs."

It's hard to figure out what to focus on for a sketch. Maybe if we had paints, I'd attempt to do the ocean. But I'm nervous about attempting ocean waves in pencil, partly because they move too much. I'd have to imagine the wave and sketch it long after it passed. So I look for something a bit more still, and decide to sketch the sea oats and the temporary fences placed to build up the sand dunes. The ocean peaks in the background to the right, but the main focus is the vertical lines of the sea oats and fencing.

The tarp works great, and the bubble wrap envelopes provide plenty of padding. In fact, I'm not sure I need all the width of the folding sit-upon now that I have a good tarp. And I miss the colorful artwork from my first design prototype. Hmm… maybe I went too far. There is still room for improvement–and one more day to execute it. Maybe my first concept was really close, and I just needed a cross-body shoulder strap, a better tarp, plus pockets to keep the bubble wrap and tarp separate from my sketchbook. That was my original design concept. I just took a shortcut for the first prototype.

Off to the side, I noticed Sue struggling with her tripod beach chair. It looked easier to unfold than her backpack beach chair, but the legs sunk down in the sand more. And Sue didn't look that comfortable sitting on it, balancing her sketch pad on her knees. But, like me, she still keeps coming up with unexpected options.

I don't know who's going to win this challenge. Sue has kept the class buzzing with each new thing she brings. They're all cool ideas, more elegant than my home-made prototypes, even if they are heavier. I'd rather carry my designs than hers. But the kids voting don't actually have to use or carry our sit-upons, so which design are they going to vote for? Sue knows *everyone*. And most of the kids who aren't her special friends still want to be on her good side. There are perks to being friends with Sue, or even noticed by Sue. At least if you're noticed in a good way. No chance of that for me now.

I guess I'm in for humiliation on Monday. So what else is new?

Chapter 40
Scrimmage

TODAY IS DOUBLE-UNDERWATER hockey day. We still have 6th period gym, but we get to do a real scrimmage after school for the first time, with 15-minute halves, a 3-minute break between halves and keeping score. We'll even have subs, just like at a real tournament. You can have up to 10 on a team, but only six in the water at a time. But you can sub on the fly. You just have to get out of the water on your end of the pool before a sub can replace you.

Tomorrow, the Science Fair takes up gym period.

JZ, Gigi, Margot, and I stay in the pool area after the bell rings to signal the end of the day. Jenn Liguori joins us. We seem to be the only girls.

Gigi, Josh, and I play forwards on the black team, while Jim, Brock, and that tall blond—Bryce Andrew Beauchamp,—play defensive backs. Jim whispers in my ear, "also known as BA, as in Bad Attitude." I'm not sure what to make of that. Margot also plays forward but stays on deck as a forward sub, while Endy Thompson stays on deck as a back sub. They will watch the play and sub in as soon as one of us comes out. It's a judgment call. You push yourself hard, and when you need a breather, you sub out to get someone with fresh legs and lungs in the game. It's especially helpful for defense because you sub out directly over your goal.

Mr. McCabe clangs the metal pipe to start play.

I play strike again, the center forward, and I beat Jenn to the puck. I make about 3 feet of forward progress when I see JZ coming in from the side to steal the puck. I curl to my left, finding Jim, and make a good pass. He swings it around to Bryce, who passes to Brock and on up to Josh.

Mark and Geoff move to cut off Josh, who curls and passes back to Brock, setting off another end-around, which ends up with Gigi streaking down the left side of the pool. I dive back down to support her drive. At the last minute, a white team forward blocks her and Gigi makes a lateral pass to me. Looking around, I see Bryce coming up behind me, while Jenn swoops down to block my pass to the goal.

I hesitate for a moment, looking for a way around Jenn. Then I hook the puck and make a backwards pass to Bryce. I stay down on the bottom to support the drive and disguise the location of the puck. Jenn sees me look to the left and moves to block me, freeing up the right for Bryce to drive to the goal. We score! We all head to the surface, giving high-fives. We swim back to our end of the pool as Mr. McCabe resets the puck at the bottom of the pool.

"That was quick thinking, Putney," Bryce compliments me as we set-up for the next point.

"You did a good job of keeping your eye on the play," Brock adds.

"Nice pass, Gigi," Jim compliments.

We keep playing like this for the rest of the half, rotating positions, seeing where we like to play. I like charging for the puck, and I'm fast, so I am happiest as a forward. But even forwards have to learn defense when your opponents break your lines. The score is pretty even by the end of the first half.

Then we change ends. Now we defend the deep end. It's only as I look across at the white team that I recognize that the person taking strike position is no longer Jenn. It's Sue Wexford.

Chapter 41

A Foul Play

WHAT IS SHE DOING here? When did she slip in? She hasn't come to a single underwater hockey session in gym period. How did she even learn how to play?

I'm so stunned by the revelation that I'm not ready when Mr. McCabe strikes the metal pipe to signal the start of play.

I swim hard towards the center of the pool then dive down for the puck, but Sue is first to the puck. She launches it over my stick and into the well.

Some pools have really deep diving wells—12 to 15 feet deep. Although this pool doesn't have a true diving well, the deep end *is* 8 feet deep. It's only 4 feet deep at the shallow end. So it takes longer to dive down to the bottom and it seems to take more energy to stay down on the bottom once you get there. And of course gravity is like an extra player, helping the puck to slide or even roll down to the bottom, making it easy to launch the puck over a defender's stick. Even just knocking the puck free can result in a long roll to the bottom of the pool. Easier for offense to support a drive. Harder for defense to clear the puck from the goal area.

So I can claim Sue just got lucky all I want, but she did still beat me to the puck. And now I'm scrambling to make up for my mistake. Luckily our backs have my back, and they are pushing the puck up the well to clear it.

Or they were, until Jenn and JZ pull a pincer move on Bryce, knocking the puck free and supporting the drive to the goal. They score easily, and it's because I missed my strike.

I *let* Sue beat me. Time to focus as we regroup before the next point.

"Was that Sue playing strike?" Jim asks. "Wow, she was super-fast, especially for a first time at strike."

"She's an amazing athlete," says Gigi.

"You seem a little winded, Putney," says Brock. "Why don't you sub out and let Margot in? Josh can take strike."

And with that, I'm replaced. My feelings are hurt, but I *am* breathing hard. I'm still in shock. I blew the point. Sue the tennis star, beat me in the water! I'm the swimmer, not her. As far as I know, anyway. Everybody swims down here. I just don't know how many swim competitively.

Maybe the best thing I can do for my team right now is to get someone with fresh legs and lungs in to take my place for a point. Backs often sub out on the fly, cause they're right there if you're defending your own goal. By the time a forward needs a sub, we're usually at the far end of the pool. It takes almost as much time and energy to sub out as it would just to catch your breath at the surface for a minute. If you stay on the surface to recover, you can still watch the play and dive back down to support your team if needed. If you sub out, you're a man down until your sub arrives… sprinting from the far end of the pool, breathing hard, even if they can at least swim on the surface and breathe through their snorkel.

The bad thing about underwater hockey is that you can't see all the details of the play developing from the pool deck. You see a lot of butts and fins on the surface—it looks a bit like a shark feeding frenzy—but the real action is on the bottom. You can only guess at the movement of the puck by ripples in the water, how the bodies on the surface maneuver, and what you can see of the action on the pool bottom.

You usually have at least three players down on the bottom at a time. That's part of the strategy… working out how to cycle between positions. You can't spend your whole team down on the bottom because eventually everyone needs to breathe. And you can't afford to have everyone on the surface at the same time.

So I watch the next point from the pool deck, trying to breathe slowly and deeply to recover my breath. Mr. McCabe clangs the gong to signal the start of the point. I watch as Josh swims out hard on the surface, then dives down to the center for the puck just as Sue dives down from the opposite side. Our two forwards follow slightly behind him, with Endy down at center back directly behind him. Jim and Brock hang back on the surface.

I watch the frenzy on the surface swing gradually to the left—Gigi's side, I think. There's a lot of thrashing towards the left wall, then suddenly everything seems to break free. The ripples circle back towards me then up the right side of the pool. I'm guessing an end-around broke the puck free and sent it to Margot with her fresh lungs and legs. We score!

Bryce and I are back in for the next point as Gigi and Jim take a breather. Across the pool, I see Sue sub out as well. I calm my breath and try to focus on the play, but I feel the pressure of defending the deep end of the pool. I want to win. This isn't just a fun match for me anymore.

For the next 10 minutes, we battle back and forth, sometimes scoring, sometimes failing to defend our goal. We rotate through our positions, giving everyone a turn to sub out and catch their breath. Josh and I tend to alternate at strike, which is the more specialized forward position. So far, I've only seen Sue at strike a couple of times.

The score is tied when Mr. McCabe clangs the metal pipe to start the last point. Josh is playing strike, and I am playing right forward for a change. Gigi is playing left forward. Opposite us, I see Jenn taking the strike position for the white team.

We swim hard for the puck. To my left, Josh dives down before me. Gigi and I follow slightly behind to the bottom. Josh beats Jenn to the puck and launches it over her stick to continue the drive. Two more white team players dive down to challenge Josh. He fakes curling to the left and passing to Gigi, drawing the white players to the left side of the pool. At the last minute he hooks the puck and passes it under his body to me.

I streak off down the right side of the pool with Brock behind me, the path to the goal temporarily clear. Just one more push I think, and I can score and end this.

I'm within 3 feet of the goal and about to crank the puck into the goal when a stick hooks my arm from behind. I've been fouled! I hear the pipe clang, and we all rise to the surface. I turn as I rise to see Sue Wexford.

A penalty shot is awarded since I was so close to the goal. Mr. McCabe walks us through the process. The offended team—that's us—gets to select two players to take the shot. The white team gets to select one person to defend the goal. The puck is placed 10 feet from the center of the goal.

The white team chooses Mark Talbot to defend the goal. Brock and I take the penalty shot. I wish I could focus, but I'm still steaming from Sue's foul.

We dive to the bottom, Brock on my left. Mark carefully keeps his hand on the pool wall as he dives too.

Then I take the puck. Just as I crank to pass to Brock, Mark charges in, hooking the puck and sliding it past me to his left, my right. And he's off, streaking down the pool, well into the safe zone.

He has defended the goal.

Sue won. Her strategy paid off. She robbed me of my goal and won.

And this was the first game she ever bothered to come to.

Mr. McCabe clangs the metal pipe and signals the end of play. Time has run out. It should have been a victory for the black team, but we end in a tie.

"I can't believe Sue robbed me of that goal, and then I blew the penalty shot," I say as I wrap a towel around myself on the pool deck. "And it's the first time she's ever played. How can she be that good?"

"It was a smart play," said Brock.

"It's the only shot she had to prevent that goal," adds Jim.

"Sue's pretty smart. She's had to learn strategy and tactics playing tennis," says Gigi. "Plus you know she's an amazing athlete, right?"

"The first question she asked about underwater hockey was about strategy," says Brock. "And it's not her first time playing.

Chapter 42
Finishing Touches

I WALK BACK HOME with Margot, Jim, and Jenn, fuming about Sue. I have to beat her in the design challenge now. I *have* to. I've already thought about my next design tweak, but I need to finish my volcano first. The paint will need time to dry.

Once home, I take the volcano out back to the patio and begin painting. I use acrylic paints. Icy blue white peaks to represent a snow cap. Black brown sides lower down, transitioning to a forest green at the lower slopes.

I check the time. Still about an hour before dinner. I take a new Tyvek tote and carefully rip out the side seams. I rip out the top seams and remove the purple handles. This is where I'll attach the top edges of the zippers that form the inside pockets made from clear plastic patterning scrim.

Then I grab some pattern scrim, zipper by the yard, a couple zipper pulls, D-rings, nylon webbing, and get to work on version 4.

I lay out the tote and cut some pattern scrim about

an inch longer than needed. I'll need to fold the edges under to create nice edges to sew onto the zippers.

This time, the scrim pockets cover what will be the entire inside of the tote, so installing the zippers is a bit trickier. I'm basically sewing a tube of fabric together–stiff Tyvek on the outer half, scrim on the inner half, with zippers connecting the two pieces. It's a bit of a challenge to get the last side of the zipper attached, but I manage. Then it's just attaching D-rings and sewing side seams.

Last step—I turn the tote right-side out. I already have a shoulder strap I can attach to the D-rings.

I weigh my final design—about 13 ounces. Under a pound. I love it! Here's a final sketch. It doesn't look a lot different from my first prototype on Tuesday, except the shoulder strap is a lot more functional. But I'm going to appreciate having those pockets to store the bubble wrap envelope and the tarp.

It's not as high tech as anything Sue will bring in, but it's super-lightweight and functional. I love having the artwork back. It's me.

After dinner, the paint dry, I insert my black volcanic rocks at the bottom, painted with swirls and hieroglyphics. I "borrow" some Romanesco broccoli to represent forested areas in the foothills. This is a dry-run, so I figure out where to put it and how much to use. I cut the Romanesco to form an exotic forest on one side of the volcano.

Then I take photographs of everything, so I can reassemble it quickly at school.

Now time for the final flame test. I suspend a makeshift bowl of aluminum foil from two bamboo skewers over the top of the glass vase. I put half the remaining strontium chloride in the foil bowl, add some rubbing alcohol, and light it with a match. The red flame is nice, but the aluminum foil spoils the effect of the volcano.

I decide to go with just the dry ice volcano. For artistic reasons. But I pack the strontium chloride up just in case I change my mind.

Decision made, I carefully wrap up the Romanesco and place it in a marked ziplock bag in the back of the refrigerator. The note reads, "DO NOT EAT UNDER PAIN OF DEATH—RESERVED FOR SCIENCE PROJECT—PUTNEY."

Then I head upstairs to try out one of Sam's virtual

reality games. I've always wanted to be Aquaman, able to breathe underwater. So Sam takes me zooming around a coral reef in the Caribbean Sea, swimming with green sea turtles and a pod of dolphins. I drift off to sleep, smiling.

Chapter 43
Exhibit Set-up

I SLEEP SOUNDLY, exhausted from playing underwater hockey. Gradually, I notice a tickling sensation by my nose. As I turn to itch it, I become aware of a rhythmic beat. Sam. The alarm didn't wake me, so she is tickling my face with her tail. Effective.

I bolt upright as I realize what day it is, throwing Sam off-balance and onto the pillow. "Sorry!" I whisper. Although I know Mom would never let me oversleep, I had hoped to wake early today.

I dress quickly and start to head downstairs when I pause to do a quick caterpillar check. Another monarch caterpillar has gone missing, and the one that was hanging in a J position from the scented geranium has already pupated. I missed it! A jade green chrysalis with gold accents hangs from the underside of a stiff geranium leaf.

No time now, but I'm going to have to figure out a better solution for my caterpillars. Thank goodness it's Friday! Maybe I can figure out something over the weekend.

Breakfast is orange juice, bacon, and eggs. I eat quickly and leave the table to boil water for the thermos. Then I head upstairs to grab my backpack and *eye*Pad.

"Sam!" I whisper.

"Yes, Putney?" Sam comes around the corner from the ceiling beams and climbs onto the *eye*Pad.

"Absolutely no running around and leaving the *eye*Pad today. I don't want to risk anyone seeing you, okay?"

Sam turns her head away from me, her tail curling around her. "I'll miss all the fun," she murmurs, looking down. A memory comes back to me. I remember how I sat, hunched over my math book, unhearing and unseeing after the sting of Sue's comments. Sam is feeling rejected.

"How about I set you up to video the experiment? Won't that give you a pretty good view of things?" I suggest as a compromise.

She perks up at this and runs to her spot on the back of the *eye*Pad, morphing into a 2D anole. I carefully pack her in my backpack and head downstairs.

I fill a thermos with the boiled water and carefully pack it in an IKEA bag, along with the thermos of dry ice, and the container of Romanesco. I pack it in an insulated lunch bag with a blue ice pack to keep it fresh. I pack my Kodiak rocks in a plastic bag and put them in the bottom of my backpack.

Mom has to drive me to school today—the volcano

is too bulky for me to carry all that way. We load the volcano in the car. Then we're off.

"Do you want any help carrying your stuff in and setting up?" asks Mom. "You did a beautiful job on that volcano. I can't wait to see it all assembled."

"Thanks, Mom. I could really use some help with the doors," I say. It's about all I can do to carry the volcano with my backpack on my shoulders and the IKEA bag on my left arm. But I really don't want Sue Wexford to see my mother helping me with my experiment, even if I could use the help. I guess I have an independent streak… partially built up out of self-defense from living with two older brothers. "Show no weakness" is my motto.

It's not far from the car to the doors, but I do have to go up a few steps. Mom holds the door open for me and I glide in. "Thanks, Mom!"

I HEAD TOWARD the multi-purpose room. I am one of the first students to arrive. Mrs. Roberts sits at a table outside the room.

"Good morning, Putney. What is your exhibit?"

"It's a volcano," I say as I twist around to give her a better view.

"Choose any spot on one of the interior tables," she instructs me. "The tables along the walls are reserved for 2D exhibits for the art fair. All the spots are numbered. Once you set up, you can come back here and get an entry form."

"Where do I hand them in?" I ask.

"There are two boxes inside, one for the science fair, one for the art exhibit. There's a place to indicate your location, name of exhibit, and your name. Mr. DiPilla and Mr. Shelley are inside and can answer any questions."

"Thank you, Mrs. Roberts."

"You're welcome. Good luck, Putney."

I WANDER INSIDE the multi-purpose room, glancing around to take in the set-up. Gigi is already inside, setting up in the front row.

"Hey Putney! How'd yours come out?" she calls to me. "Want to set up by me?"

"Sure," I say, smiling. I head over to the spot next to hers, setting my volcano down on the table. I set the IKEA bag down and take my backpack off, and start pulling out my rocks to place around the base. My volcano has a white peak, with charcoal grey slopes, blending into my dark charcoal gray volcanic Kodiak rocks at the bottom. I'll wait until just before judging to place the bright green Romanesco around the slope to the right.

We head out to Mrs. Roberts to grab entry forms, then head back to our spots. There are tent cards to write out our experiment title on. The back side is for our name.

"DID YOU DECIDE to just enter the science fair?" asks

Gigi.

"Well... Mrs. Roberts said we could only have one entry," I hedge. "But I kind of hoped I could enter this in both exhibits. Can you help me snag an extra entry form when Mrs. Roberts isn't looking?"

"Piece of cake," laughs Gigi. "She knows how bad my writing can be. I'll just say I messed up and need an extra form."

"Awesome! Thanks so much," I call out in relief as she heads back out to grab an extra form for me.

Ten minutes later, I have two forms filled out, one for the science fair and one for the art exhibit. I slip them into the two entry form boxes, and we head over to homeroom.

CHATTER FILLS the classroom as students start to congregate. The bell rings and we all settle down in our seats.

Mr. DiPilla reads the announcements. "The science fair/art exhibit will be judged during 6th period. You'll be given a slip with a time for judging on it. Please be by your station at least 10 minutes early, and wait until the panel of judges dismisses you. Then you'll be free to look at the other exhibits. Any questions?"

"When will the winners be announced?" asks Sue Wexford.

"Winners will be announced at the end of 6th period," replies Mr. DiPilla. "Good luck!"

Chapter 44
Round 4

IN SCIENCE CLASS, we learn about acids and bases, and use a universal solution like litmus paper to tell whether a solution is acidic (red or pink color), neutral (green color) or a base (blue color). We have a beaker with a weak base in it that turns the universal solution blue. As we add drops of the acidic solution using pipettes, we watch as the color changes to green, then yellow, and finally pink. It's fun and doesn't take a lot of concentration.

When the bell rings at the end of science class, I rush to my locker to get my final sit-upon prototype. I feel nauseous as I head into art class, remembering Sue's personal foul in underwater hockey and her endless stream of high-tech prototypes. Who will win? And what will my fate be?

This time, a lime green padded seat is sitting on top of a table. Sue stands beside it, smirking. She's surrounded by half the class, as usual.

The bell rings and Mr. Shelley asks us to take our seats.

"All right, this is it, time to show off your final prototypes for the sit-upon design challenge," he says. "Please put your sit-upon on the table in front of you. Looks like we have a couple new or old entries today, and we'll take a look at them before taking votes."

"Miss Wexford, would you like to share what you brought today and why you selected it?"

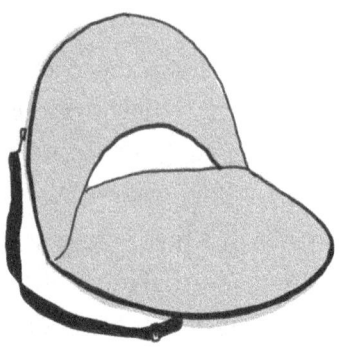

"It's called a stadium seat, and it weighs just about four pounds, so a pound lighter than my tripod chair yesterday. It's waterproof, has a back pocket, and should be stable on any flat surface. Plus, it's more comfortable to sit on, and I decided there were some advantages to being on the ground—easier to spread out my supplies," responds Sue.

"Nice entry," compliments Mr. Shelley. "Miss Hicks, would you like to share your latest design?"

"After using my folding sit-upon prototype with the tarp, I realized it was heavier than I needed if I were going to use a tarp, anyway. And I loved the artwork on my bag. But my original concept included interior pockets and a cross-body shoulder strap. So I went back to that and made it the way I originally envisioned. But I kept the waterproof tarp. It weighs less than a pound now and still holds my sketch pad and pencils."

"Well done, both of you," says Mr. Shelley. "Do we have any other new entries?"

Mr. Shelley paused a moment, then continues, "All right, here's the plan. I'm passing out sheets of white paper. Please take one and write your name on it, then name your design. You can list any features. We'll take 5 minutes for everyone to look at all the designs before we head out to sketch the ocean again. Take this time to think about which one you'd want to carry and use in the field for sketching."

"When we get back, I'll hand out an adhesive dot to everyone. You'll have one last chance to walk around, look at the designs, and ask any questions you want. When you're ready, you'll vote for your favorite by putting your adhesive dot on the white paper for that design. The winner will be the one with the most dots."

WE HEAD BACK out to the beach for another day of sketching. But I probably spend about half of that time walking around, looking at the other designs, and answering questions from others who want to see my design.

Sue seems more comfortable on her stadium seat than she did on the tripod chair. But it still looks huge to carry. But I have to admit, it did work great on the sand.

JZ's sit-upon looks lighter than it did the other day.

"Did you do something to your design?" I ask.

"Just a minor tweak," she admits. "I stole your idea and used a bubble wrap envelope to make it lighter. You're right—it's enough padding, and it makes it so much lighter."

After half an hour, Mr. Shelley herds us back to class.

"ANY QUESTIONS or observations about any of the designs that you would like to share?" asks Mr. Shelley as he passes out the adhesive voting dots.

"Yeah," I say, raising my hand. "JZ's improved her design. She made it lighter by using a bubble-wrap envelope."

"Nice job, Miss Sparrow," says Mr. Shelley. "You leveraged an idea from a classmate."

"Isn't that cheating?" asks Lynne Smythe-Dixon.

"Not at all," laughs Mr. Shelley. "It's called recognizing a great idea, and leveraging it to your own design. There's nothing patented about the use of bubble wrap envelopes in sit-upons. So there's no infringement. This whole exercise was intended to get you to learn from experience to improve your designs. You don't have to learn just from your own experience.

"Any other questions?" He pauses, looking around

the room. "All right, you have 5 minutes to examine the designs and vote."

We get up, milling around the room. Although I like my design best, I think it's bad manners to vote for myself, so I look at all the designs. I still like JZ's French bistro scene sit-upon with the duct-taped seams and handle. It's cute and clever and didn't require any sewing. It doesn't hold her sketch pad. But she did tweak it when she switched to a bubble wrap envelope. She gets my vote.

I hang back now, watching the other kids vote. Sue's posse all vote for her, but I don't see Sue vote… at least not yet. I'm trying not to look to see who votes for me and who votes for Sue. I kinda don't want to know. But I do want to know who Sue votes for.

Then I see Lynne sidle up next to Sue. Sue hands Lynne her dot. Then Lynne makes another pass around the table and puts the dot on Sue's paper. Hmm. I guess it is okay to vote for yourself. Indirectly.

AFTER MR. SHELLEY confirms that everyone has finished voting, he counts up the number of dots on each paper. There are only four with multiple dots—mine, Sue's, JZ's, and one of the garbage bag/newspaper basic designs with a drawstring handle.

"Well done all of you. You've exceeded my expectations for this design challenge. And now I'd like to congratulate our winner in a very tight race… Miss Hicks," announces Mr. Shelley.

Applause breaks out, and Gigi, Margot, JZ, and Jim give me high-fives.

The bell rings, and I head out of class, smiling. I have the whole weekend to figure out what to have Sue do for me next Monday. But I still have the science fair/art exhibit to get through first.

As we head out of the room and into math, I am floating on cloud nine. One big challenge down, one to go.

I'VE COME CRASHING BACK to earth by the time lunch time arrives, my stomach full of butterflies. My mind drifts to my dry ice and hot water thermos bottles. What if I don't have enough dry ice left?

Over lunch, Margo suggests we have a picnic lunch at the beach Saturday.

"It will be nice to celebrate the end of the first week of classes, and we can play Boules and frisbee and swim in the ocean," Margot suggests.

At least one of us can think of life beyond the science fair/art show.

Chapter 45

A Complication

SOMEHOW I GET THROUGH English and social studies. As the bell for 6th period rings, I grab my backpack and head into the multi-purpose room to finish staging my exhibit.

I have tunnel vision as I focus on setting the final touches on my exhibit, barely glancing around the room. I have 10 minutes before my assigned judging time, and I need to focus. It only takes a few minutes to arrange the Romanesco broccoli on toothpicks that I press into the styrofoam section around the base. It makes a lush green forest, which happens to be edible. Then I set the thermos of hot water and the thermos of dry ice next to the volcano, along with a pair of tongs.

Next to me, Gigi gasps in horror. Her dish of baking soda has disappeared. It's only then that I notice our tent cards have been switched. We are both doing volcano projects. Someone sabotaged her project, probably thinking it was my project. I can't imagine who switched the tent cards, but I can guess who removed the baking soda.

"Are you missing anything else?" I ask. "Do you still have the vinegar?"

Gigi sticks a finger in the bottle of vinegar on her table to taste it. "It's vinegar, all right," she says. "But what am I going to do about the baking soda?"

"Wait here," I say. "Maybe I can find some from the kitchen or the General Store."

I grab my backpack and head into the restroom, picking the large handicap stall in the back. No time to waste, I get out my *eye*Pad and ask Sam to print me some baking soda. I dump the strontium chloride from my glass bowl into the plastic wrap and put the empty bowl on the bottom of the case.

"You realize what you're doing," she says. "You know the consequences."

"I have the ability to help a friend," I say. "She doesn't deserve to be humiliated. She's had my back from the first day. Now I have an opportunity to repay her. I want to do this."

Barely 30 seconds later, I have a small glass bowl full of baking soda, and one of the magic reservoir lights has gone out. But it's for Gigi. She's worth it.

I rush back into the Multi-Purpose room, handing Gigi the glass container with baking soda. The relief that floods her face is all the thanks I need.

I take a deep breath, and check that my hot water is still hot, or at least warm enough to melt dry ice, and that my dry ice is still—dry ice. Next I set my *eye*Pad on the table to video the experiment. Gigi helps me find a good angle. Satisfied with the effect, I dart to the wall by the door to drop off my backpack with the others, then return to my station to await judging.

We will have to give a brief presentation, so I go over a few notes I printed on an index card. Then I wait.

Chapter 46

Judging

Next to me, Gigi's volcano goes off without a hitch. I smile at her, then a frog climbs into my throat as the judges turn to me.

"What do we have here?" asks Mr. DiPilla. Mr. Shelley and two other teachers I don't know form the team of judges.

"This is a dry ice volcano," I explain as I open the thermos with hot water and pour it into the glass vase.

"As you know, there are three main phases of matter: solids, liquids, and gases. You can alter the phase of many substances by raising or lowering its temperature. Water is a liquid at room temperature. If you boil it, it will turn into a gas—steam. If you freeze it, it turns into ice. Even metals can be liquified by heating them in a crucible. It takes a lot of heat—thousands of degrees—but that's how materials engineers make special alloys. The metal is melted until it makes a kind of soup, then different elements are added. Next the molten metal is poured into some sort of form or casting mold to cool and solidify.

"The normal progression of phases is solid to liquid to gas, or the reverse. It is unusual to skip a phase, but it can happen. The phase at room temperature depends on the substance. Water is a liquid, carbon dioxide is a gas, steel is a solid.

"Dry ice is frozen carbon dioxide. What's unusual about it is that it changes from a solid directly to a gas, skipping the liquid phase." Now I open the remaining thermos and pull out a chunk of dry ice using the tongs and carefully drop it into the hot water.

"The fog that is coming out of the volcano is carbon dioxide gas. It's heavier than air, so it sinks to the ground. It's often used in theatre, TV, and movies for dramatic effect. But its most useful function is to pack food for shipping. It keeps things colder than ice. But, the real advantage it has over ice is that the package doesn't get soggy when it melts. Cardboard loses its strength when it gets wet.

"This dry ice came from Alaska and was used to pack a box of salmon we caught earlier this year, and this is Romanesco broccoli that we grew in Alaska," I say, and point to the bright green Romanesco.

"Tell me more about the… broccoli?" asks one of the unknown teachers.

"Romanesco broccoli, or just Romanesco. Alaska has really great weather for growing vegetables in the broccoli family. Romanesco has grown in Italy since the 1600s. Most grocery stores just don't carry it. It's a member of the same family, but is so unusual in looks.

I think it has something to do with the Fibonacci number, or fractals. It's my favorite vegetable."

"Those are interesting rocks," notes Mr. Shelley. "Tell me about them."

"Well, in Kodiak, we paint rocks and leave them on trails for others to find. These are rocks from Jewel beach. They're volcanic rocks, so I thought they'd be appropriate staging for a volcano exhibit. I painted designs to represent ocean waves, fish, lizards, birds, and plants. I used a few Zentangle patterns as well. I looked at pictures of petroglyphs and hieroglyphics for inspiration, and decided I wanted to keep my rock designs as line work… white lines on the charcoal grey rocks. So the designs are all different, but have the same feel," I conclude.

"What media did you use?" asks Mr. Shelley.

"This is just white acrylic paint, mixed with a bit of water and gloss media. It takes a bit of practice to manage a thin line, but it's waterproof," I answer.

"Yes it is," affirms Mr. Shelley. "It dries very quickly and is permanent. That's very nice work, Putney."

"Thank you, Putney," says Mr. DiPilla. "That's a very creative exhibit."

I let out a breath I didn't know I was holding, relieved to be finished with the presentation. I follow Gigi and Margot, and we wander around the room to view the other exhibits. Art exhibits range from tempura paintings to prints and a few watercolors. As we round the corner to another row of science exhibits, my heart stops.

Straight ahead is another volcano exhibit. Around it are some very familiar black rocks with painted designs. My designs. My heart thumps loudly in my chest.

"Gigi," I whisper. "What do I do now?"

Just then, Sam materializes on my shoulder and whispers in my ear. "Putney, quick! Someone has planted a gold necklace in your backpack. I think you're about to be framed for theft."

Like an idiot, I stand like a deer frozen in headlights as Sue Wexford takes her place behind her volcano as the judging panel arrives. It's a traditional baking soda and vinegar volcano. Sue has a candle suspended at the top and holds a flat wooden stick with metallic salts at the top. I guess it's supposed to burn a different color, but it just looks like a normal yellow flame to me.

Mr. Shelley whispers something to Mr. DiPilla, then addresses Sue. "Those are interesting rocks. Can you tell us about them?"

Sue beams as she replies, "These are authentic Kodiak Trail Rocks. They're volcanic rocks and the latest thing here. I bought them at Sheik Boutique and thought they'd give an aura of an authentic volcano."

Well, I guess Ms. Tempura must have sold some of my rocks. I just never expected to see them at my science fair.

I watch as Lynne Smythe-Dixon squeezes in next to Sue and whispers something in her ear. Sue looks straight up and catches my eye. There's a cold gleam in her eye as she points to me and says, "Putney cheated. Anyone can buy those rocks at Sheik Boutique. She can't use that for an original art exhibit. She's a thief and a cheat."

Chapter 47
Mission Impossible

"WHAT?" I manage to choke out. I am frozen like a deer in headlights.

"Not only is she a cheat, but she stole my necklace."

"No," I stammer. "I painted those rocks. I have proof."

"MOVE," Sam hisses in my ear.

This time, I am able to get my feet moving. My *eye*Pad has all the proof I need about my Kodiak trail rocks. But what am I going to do about the necklace?

"Any ideas?" I ask Sam as I round the corner to our table. My backpack is just across the aisle. Next to it, I recognize a watermelon Fossil backpack that belongs to Sue Wexford. I hear footsteps behind me. I am out of time.

"If I only had more time to switch the necklace back," I mutter to Sam.

"Hang on," says Sam. "I've got an idea… extended virtual reality mode. Not quite freezing time, but the effect should be the same for people within about 20 feet of you. When I say go… GO! I should be able to give you about 15 seconds."

"Pick up the *eye*Pad," Sam instructs. "The necklace is in the top center key pocket."

I obey.

"GO!"

Fifteen, fourteen, Sam gives me a countdown in my mind as I dart across the aisle to my backpack, *eye*Pad in hand. *Thirteen, twelve*, I'm unzipping the key pocket. *Eleven, ten*, I'm searching for the necklace. *Nine, eight*, found it! *Seven, six*, I've zipped my backpack up. *Five, four*, pivoting on my knee, I drop the necklace into Sue's backpack, not fussy about where I put it. *Three, two*, I spring up and cross the aisle back to my exhibit. *One*, I look up, my *eye*Pad in my hand by my volcano. Time seems to speed up, as Mr. Shelley and Mr. Drewes round the corner.

Sam coaches me on what to do. "Just show them the receipt for the Kodiak trail rocks," she instructs. "Remember, you know nothing about the theft of any necklace because you didn't do it. Pull up the receipt for the trail rocks now and show it to Mr. Shelly." With that, she runs down my arm and morphs back into the *eye*Pad.

Mr. Shelley reaches me just as I pull up the receipt on my *eye*Pad. Gigi is right behind him.

MR. HAUCK, the principal, is called upon to settle the issue. One of the teachers, Mr. Drewes, puts his hand on my shoulder and guides me to the back of the room. He asks me which backpack is mine. I point to the orange one, also with painted swirls on it, just like some of my rocks. It's unique, made from an old Coast Guard dry suit.

Gigi comes up behind us and addresses Mr. Hauck, saying, "Putney is telling the truth. I took her to Sheik Boutique to meet Ms. Tempura. She took several rocks on consignment. Just ask her. She'll tell you. I can give you her phone number."

"That may be," Mr. Hauck replies, "but we have to investigate this charge of theft first. Then we'll sort out the story behind the rocks." He instructs Mr. Drewes to search my backpack.

One by one, he checks each pocket, then shakes his head. "There's nothing here," he confirms.

"That's impossible!" Sue Wexford comes up behind him. "I saw her do it. It should be right in the center pocket. Check again!" she says, pointing to the pocket of interest.

Mr. Shelley searches this time and holds the backpack for everyone to see.

"Which backpack is yours, Miss Wexford?" asks Mr. Hauck.

"It's the one just to the left," says Sue, pointing.

"Mr. Drewes, will you please search Miss Wexford's backpack?" Mr. Hauck asks.

After a minute of searching, Mr. Drewes reaches in and pulls out the beautiful gold necklace that Sue was wearing on Monday.

I let out a deep breath. Gigi materializes beside me.

What else does Sue have? The rocks.

Knowing Sue, my guess is offense. Right on cue, I hear her shout, "What about the rocks? They're from Sheik Boutique. They can't count as an original art exhibit."

I turn to Mr. Hauck and say, "My rocks are not from Sheik Boutique. Anyway, those rocks are my rocks that Sheik Boutique is selling. I've got the proof right here on my tablet." I pull up the signed receipt and photo of the rocks left on consignment at Sheik Boutique.

A moment later, we all head back to Sue's exhibit to examine the rocks in her exhibit against the receipt and photo from Miss Tempura at Sheik Boutique.

It's clear that Sue's rocks are among them. Gigi backs me up. JZ and Margot appear at my side. They entered the Art Exhibit, staged against the back wall. They didn't catch all the drama of Sue's meltdown.

"Well, I think that exonerates Putney of all charges," says Mr. Hauck. "Judges, I believe you have a few science exhibits to finish judging, then the art exhibits." Then he adds, "Miss Wexford, will you please accompany me to my office?"

Chapter 48

Meltdown

I FEEL VERY FAINT. I need to get away from all the prying eyes. "Mrs. Roberts?" I ask. "I don't feel very well. Is it okay if I go outside to get some air?"

"Yes, I suppose that would be all right. Just don't go very far." She pauses for a moment, thinking. "Why don't you wait in the pool area? I'll send someone to get you before they announce the results of the judging." Then, turning to JZ and Margot she adds, "I don't think she needs three escorts. Do you?"

"Moral support," says JZ.

Mrs. Roberts looks sternly at her. "Has your exhibit been judged yet?"

JZ looks away. "Well then, go back to your exhibit. You can join your friends in the pool area after your judging is complete." Turning to Margot, "That goes for you, too, Miss French."

"Yes, Mrs. Roberts," they chorus.

"I'll look after her," Gigi volunteers, and we head out the door. "Come and join us when your judging is finished."

The pool area is in front of the building, before the parking lot. There's a lot of landscaping around it, making a private oasis and providing some shade—depending on the time of day. Tall trees shelter the pool from view of the walking path. It's early afternoon, so they don't cast a long shadow yet, just a shady corner by the side of the pool.

"Let's dangle our feet in the pool," suggests Gigi.

"Sounds good. And I could use a little water on my face right about now," I say.

We kick off our shoes, dangle our legs in the water. I splash a little water on my face and lean back. I don't understand what happened. I can see how the lasagna incident got me on her radar, and everything seemed to escalate from there. But accusing someone of theft and planting a necklace seems a bit extreme. Is she really that sore about losing the sit-upon design challenge?

I've never been accused of being a thief before. My heartbeat is still racing. My face still feels hot.

"JZ will be doing recon," says Gigi. "You just wait. If there's any scuttlebutt, she'll get it."

I glance over at the building in time to see Margot sliding out the door. She joins us by the side of the pool.

"What's up with Sue?" I ask. "Is there always this much drama around her?"

"She's sort of used to being the center of attention," Margot says.

"I think she's having a really tough time at home," Gigi adds. "She really does have a lot of natural tennis talent, and her parents have signed her up with a top coach. She's under a lot of pressure to do well. But her dad works crazy hours as a top sports medicine surgeon and her mom is one of the top realtors on the island. They're always working, and they expect so much of her."

"What does she do for fun?" I ask.

"Shop," chuckles Margot. "But I think it's usually with her friends. I don't think her mom has a lot of time for her."

"I think she really does love tennis, but it's still a lot of pressure," adds Gigi.

JUST THEN, JZ appears at the door and waves us over. We quickly dry our feet, put on our shoes, and join JZ at the door.

"First, I'm supposed to tell you it's almost time to announce the winners," says JZ.

"What else?" asks Margot.

"Well, I just heard some rumors that Sue's parents may be breaking up," says JZ.

"That's rough," I say.

Reluctantly, we head back to the chaos and bustle of the science fair/art exhibit.

THERE'S A LOUD BUZZ in the room as we head inside. It seems rather dim after the bright sunshine outside. The judges huddle in a corner. Mr. Hauck consults with them.

Then the huddle breaks, and Mr. Hauck walks over to the front of the room. "May I have your attention, please," his voice booms over the microphone.

"I would like to announce the winners of the art exhibit," he continues. "Most creative use of tempura goes to Josh Teague." Applause follows.

"Most original print goes to JZ Sparrow." I whoop with joy and pat JZ on the back.

"Most imaginative watercolor goes to Brittany James." More cheers.

"Now for the winners of the science exhibit," he continues. "Best robot goes to Brock Hudson." Applause breaks out.

"Best volcano goes to Gigi Hernandez." My heart plummets a tiny bit. But I'm really happy for Gigi. I give another big whoop and a big hug. I am so lucky to have her for a friend.

"Best collection goes to Jim Liguori." Another round of applause.

As much as I wished to come away with some award, it feels like a major victory to be standing right now. I am so grateful to have found friends like Gigi, JZ, and Margot my first week of school. There will be other projects and other exhibits.

"And now for our Grand Prize winner," he continues. "Best of Show, for a very creative dual entry papier-mâché sculpture and dry ice volcano goes to

Putney Hicks!"

I feel my cheeks turn pink and tears prick my eyes as Gigi, JZ, and Margot clap me on the back and hug me. They push me forward to accept my award. I see Sam pivoting slightly to capture the moment on video.

Out of the corner of my eye, I see Sue Wexford in the doorway. I can't quite make out the look on her face. Determination? Then a sudden change of focus as she turns her head towards something. Is that a look of surprise on her face? I follow the angle of her gaze and my heart nearly stops. She's looking at Sam. My tablet. My somewhat magical tablet that just pivoted on its own to videotape me getting my award. Uh oh… I wonder what next week will bring.

Just then, Mr. Hauck's voice booms over the loudspeaker. "Just one quick announcement before you're all dismissed. Next Friday, before Labor Day Weekend, we will host a Float-a-Boat Regatta. Entries will be open to teams of five or six. Your objective will be to design, build, and test a cardboard boat. Have a good weekend!"

The bell rings, and we head out into the sultry August heat.

Epilogue

I TWIST MY FINGERS as I consider what I am asking Sam to do, and what it will cost. Is it worth it?

But Sue's snide remarks haunt me, stabbing me with pain and doubt.

What if I will never be as good as anything she can buy? What if my dreams really are… silly? unrealistic?

It's strange how uplifting some words can be, and how poisonous others can be. And I tend to be a bit obsessive… so it's easier for the bad stuff to replay over and over until it takes root.

One question, one magic power level. If I do this, I'll have used two of Sam's 10 power reserves.

What would you do? If you could ask your future self just one question, would you? And what would your question be?

I turn to Sam and say, "I want to do this."

Curie rubs against my leg and purrs.

Sam instructs me to push the four screw-like things in the corners of the *eye*Pad case in the clockwise direction, starting with the one to the left of the home button, and to repeat this five times.

The beams form a point above the surface of the *eye*Pad, but this time a head appears. It's me, but 50 years older. My hair is still long, but it looks blonder now, with some gray streaked in it.

"Hello Putney, hello Sam, it's so good to see you again. And Curie, too," my older self says, smiling at me. Her eyes, my eyes, crinkling at the corners.

"Ask your question… I know you've thought about it long and hard."

"Does it make a difference? My design work. All the things I dream up and make, like my sit-upon, my backpack, and my mesh tide-pooling baskets? Or is Sue right and I'll never amount to anything?"

My 62-year-old self smiles back at me and says, "It made all the difference in the world. Maybe you're just beginning to understand why. It's an amazing feeling, isn't it? When you come up with an idea and can create something to solve a need you've identified. To do the whole design cycle–plan-do-check-act. Design and make. Evaluate and tweak.

"It's like giving birth—creating something new. And learning how to learn, how to improve. Learning that mistakes and failures just help us get better, smarter, and more effective the next time.

"I learned, *we learned*, how to be resilient. We learned how to manage projects, even learned a bit of industrial engineering… how to set up an efficient workspace. We did it by *doing*. We boosted our initiative, creativity, and self-confidence. And it still gives me great joy to create new things. Just like you're doing now."

"But how did it make a difference?" I ask.

My 62-year-old self sighs, then answers with a gentle smile, "I had to choose between art and engineering for a career. I chose engineering. But it was hard. When I got my first D ever during sophomore year, I really questioned whether I'd made the right choice, whether I even *could* do it. It was the first time I seriously doubted myself. Well, maybe other than that C in Algebra I, when I finally decided I needed to ask for help."

"Back to the D," I prompt.

"That was a turning point for me. I had to choose. I really didn't know *if* I could succeed in engineering. All my life I'd been following in footsteps, just taking the next class laid out for me, not really questioning my parents or my counsellors. I never really doubted that I could succeed before that. But I'm not like Logan. I can't just roll with C's, and especially not a D. It was scary. I did not want to quit, to be a *quitter*. But I didn't want to try and then fail either.

"So I dug down deep, questioning myself. Asking myself what to do, whether I really wanted to do this, whether I *could* do this. For the first time in my life, I never knew myself."

"How did you decide?"

"I remembered all the projects I'd completed. All

the things I'd... *we'd* dreamed up and made. I knew that I was creative... I just figured I needed to learn a new medium. All those things we did in elementary school and later, all those summers creating and dreaming... that was the bedrock I latched onto. That became the foundation that gave me the confidence to go forward.

"Engineering was not an easy path for me. I had to keep choosing engineering. It was tough finishing my bachelor of science degree. But I learned to hold *myself* accountable for my learning, not a test, not a grade, not a professor. When I took responsibility for my own learning, everything changed."

"Was it worth it?"

"I'm grateful every day for the 30 plus years that I worked as an engineer. Engineers are problem-solvers. What better career for a changing world? What better skills to boost your self-confidence?

"Art will always be a part of me, a part of us. Maybe I didn't earn my living directly through my artwork, but I've always had creative hobbies and the artistic side fueled the creative problem-solving skills for my analytical engineering problems. And it still gives me joy. But engineering taught me to do hard things. When you learn to do hard things, doing hard things becomes rewarding. And those skills help get you through the challenging times in life. For me, it was the difference between taking the initiative to chart my own course instead of reacting to what others threw at me, or feeling that I had no options but to depend on someone else for everything.

"Everything is so much easier when you believe you can stand on your own two feet. It gives you choices–or the strength to look for new options. Life is toughest when you feel you don't have any options. Even if you choose a hard path, recognizing that choice makes it easier.

"So, yes, it made a difference. It made all the difference in the world. Hang in there. You're in for a pretty amazing ride."

About the Author

Marsha Tufft loves her family, dogs, butterflies, swimming, the ocean, teaching her dogs cool tricks, sewing, quilting, painting, and solving problems by coming up with her own designs. She's a retired engineer, with degrees in mechanical (BSME), aerospace (MSAsE), and materials engineering (PhD), and enjoys developing experiments targeting girls to give them fun experiences with science, engineering, and math.

Marsha also has a passion for butterflies, and has raised monarchs, black swallowtails, and zebra swallowtails from caterpillars, capturing the magical moments of metamorphosis on camera. While working on her Ph.D., she also studied aerodynamics of flapping insect flight, and has a cool experiment to show the flow field around a butterfly's clap-and-fling take-off.

Because math is so important to success in STEM fields—science, technology, engineering, and math—Marsha has fun experiments that show the magic and power of math.

Marsha blogs about her projects, designs, and STEM experiments at **www.putneydesigns.com**.

Want more Project Details?
STEM Experiments to do at home?

The STRAW TRICK explained

The Great EGG DROP Challenge

Build (and Test) a Cardboard BOAT

Build (and Test) a Cardboard CATAPULT

Butterfly FLIGHT... and cake decorating!

Plant It and They Will Come—my guide to raising

butterflies

Please visit my website,

www.putneydesigns.com

Or, sign up for my mailing list so you never miss a new book, project, or experiment! Plus, receive **exclusive character sketches**!

www.putneydesigns.com/subscribe

One last thing...

If you liked my book, could you do me a **HUGE favor** and **leave a review online?**

Your reviews make a big difference!

Or, visit my webiste and drop me a note to let me know what you thought about my story.

www.putneydesigns.com

Thanks so much!

MK Tufft

CPSIA information can be obtained
at www.ICGtesting.com
Printed in the USA
LVHW040456121120
671367LV00007B/268